"I told you I'd protect you and find the truth, and I keep my promises."

"I guess I'm not accustomed to men I can count on," she said.

Caleb rubbed the back of her neck with his thumb, and a frisson of something sweet and sensual rippled between them. "Some men actually care about family and honor, about protecting women and children."

Madelyn desperately wanted to believe him. "But you don't have a family of your own?"

Intense pain filled his eyes so quickly that it sucked the air from Madelyn's lungs. Then a shuttered look fell across his face, and he pulled away.

"I'm sorry if I said something wrong, Caleb." Madelyn touched his arm, needing to apologize, to make up for whatever she'd said to upset him, but he launched himself to his feet and slanted her a look that warned her that the conversation was over.

Madelyn missed the intimacy she'd felt between them. But he was right to keep their relationship focused on the case.

Still, the anguish in his eyes haunted her. Caleb had his own secrets. Secrets he obviously didn't want to share. Secrets that had hurt him deeply.

And for once, instead of thinking about her own pain, she wanted to alleviate his.

RITA HERRON

THE MISSING TWIN

TORONTO NEW YORK LONDON
AMSTERDAM PARIS SYDNEY HAMBURG
STOCKHOLM ATHENS TOKYO MILAN MADRID
PRAGUE WARSAW BUDAPEST AUCKLAND

To Mother for all the love she gave her own twins…

Recycling programs
for this product may
not exist in your area.

ISBN-13: 978-0-373-74605-7

THE MISSING TWIN

Copyright © 2011 by Rita B. Herron

ABOUT THE AUTHOR

Award-winning author Rita Herron wrote her first book when she was twelve, but didn't think real people grew up to be writers. Now she writes so she doesn't have to get a *real* job. A former kindergarten teacher and workshop leader, she traded her storytelling to kids for romance, and now she writes romantic comedies and romantic suspense. She lives in Georgia with her own romance hero and three kids. She loves to hear from readers, so please write her at P.O. Box 921225, Norcross, GA 30092-1225, or visit her website at www.ritaherron.com.

Books by Rita Herron

*Nighthawk Island
††Guardian Angel Investigations
**Guardian Angel Investigations: Lost and Found

CAST OF CHARACTERS

Caleb Walker—He will do anything to protect Madelyn and find her missing child—anything but lose his heart to the woman and her twins.

Madelyn Andrews—She thought one of her twin daughters died at birth. Now she has reason to believe she's alive, and she'll die herself before she'll give up her search to find her.

Sara Andrews—She knows her sister is alive and in danger. But everyone thinks she's crazy—everyone except Caleb Walker, the big Indian who can walk on fire. Will he find Cissy in time?

Cissy Andrews—She's running for her life. Can her sister, Sara, hear her cries for help?

Tim Andrews—The father of the twins abandoned Madelyn and Sara after they lost Cissy. Was he too grief-stricken to stay with them, or was he guilt-stricken instead?

Jameson Stanford Mansfield—The lawyer who handled adoptions for Dr. Emery insists he has no knowledge about the missing twin. Is he lying to protect himself?

Nadine Cotter—A nurse who consoled Madelyn the night she lost Cissy. Did Nadine know that Cissy survived?

Howard Zimmerman—The funeral director handled the memorial service. Did he cover up the fact that the casket Madelyn buried was empty?

Ava and Bill Butterworth—The child they adopted is not Madelyn's; but they may know where she is.

Rayland and Beatrice Pedderson—Someone tipped off Rayland that Caleb and Madelyn would be coming and asking questions. But Rayland Pedderson talks with his gun.

Danielle and Doug Smith—Is Smith really their last name or are they on the run?

Chapter One

Fear clogged five-year-old Sara Andrews's throat. She could see her twin sister running from the old wooden house, stumbling down the porch steps, crying as she raced toward the woods.

"Help me," Cissy cried. "He's gonna hurt Mommy!"

The wind whistled, shaking the trees. Leaves swirled and rained down. A dog howled in the distance.

Then thunder boomed.

No, not thunder.

It was the big, hulking man storming down the steps. "Cissy!" the monster bellowed. "Come back here."

He slapped at the branches with his beefy fists, moving so fast he was nearly on top of her. Then he lunged for her.

Cissy screamed and darted to the right, running, running, running into the darkness....

The monster reached a pawlike hand toward her and snatched her jacket. Cissy screamed again, stumbled and fell to the ground. But her jacket slid off in the man's hands, and he cursed.

Sweat slid down Sara's temple. Her heart was pounding so loud she could hear it beating in her ears. "Get up," Sara whispered. "Get up and run, Cissy."

As if Cissy heard her, she took a deep breath, grabbed a fistful of dirt and hurled it at the man.

The dust sprayed his eyes and he cursed, then swung one fist toward Cissy. Cissy dodged the blow, pushed herself to her hands and knees and stood. Tree branches cracked. The wind screeched.

The monster roared and dove for her.

"No!" Sara cried. "Run, Cissy, run."

Tears streamed down her sister's cheeks as Cissy tried to run, but the monster yanked her by the hair and dragged her back toward the house.

"Help me!" Cissy cried. "Please, help me!"

"No!" Sara screamed. "Let her go...."

MADELYN ANDREWS raced toward her daughter's bedroom, her lungs tightening at the sound of her daughter's terrified sobs. Outside, the wind roared off the mountain and sleet pelted the window, reminding her that a late winter storm raged around the small town of Sanctuary, North Carolina.

Shivering with the cold, she threw open the door, flipped on the sunflower lamp Sara had begged for and crossed the distance to her little girl's bed. Sara was thrashing around, tangled in the bright green comforter, sobbing and shaking.

"No, don't hurt her, don't hurt Cissy…"

Madelyn's heart broke, worry throbbing inside her as she eased herself onto the mattress and gently shook Sara.

"Honey, wake up. It's just a nightmare," she whispered. Although Sara would insist that it was real.

Sara sobbed harder, swinging out her hands as if fighting off an invisible monster, and Madelyn pulled her into her arms. Tears blurred her own eyes as she rocked her back and forth. "Shh, honey, Mommy's here. It's all right."

"Gonna hurt Mommy…" Sara wailed. "Help Cissy. We have to help Cissy!"

"Shh, baby." Madelyn stroked Sara's fine, blond hair. "No one is going to hurt Mommy. I'm right here."

Sara jerked her eyes open, her pupils distorted, her lower lip quivering. For a moment, she stared at Madelyn as if she didn't recognize her.

"But Cissy's mommy is hurt," Sara said in a shaky voice. "The bad man chased Cissy into the woods and he catched her, and…"

"It was a dream." Madelyn cupped Sara's face between her hands, imploring her to believe her. "A really bad dream, sweetheart, but it was just a nightmare."

"No," Sara choked out. "It was real. Cissy's in trouble and we gots to help her or he's gonna hurt her…"

"Oh, honey," Madelyn said softly.

Sara gulped. "It *was* real, Mommy. I saw Cissy." Tears rolled down her face. "And she saw me. She begged me to help her. I tolded her to get up and run, but he caught her and dragged her back to the house.…"

Shaken by the horror in Sara's voice, Madelyn took a deep breath, desperately trying to calm the anxiety bleeding through her.

She dried Sara's tears with her fingers. "Sara, I told you that we lost Cissy a long time ago."

"No," Sara said with a firm shake of her head. "She lives with that other mommy. But if we don't helps her, that mean man's gonna kill 'em both."

Madelyn hugged Sara to her, lost in turmoil.

Something was very wrong with her little girl. She'd been having these nightmares for the past two months, ever since they'd moved back to Sanctuary, and nothing Madelyn had done or said had helped. Not her long talks with her about Cissy, Sara's twin who they'd lost at birth, or the therapists Madelyn had consulted for assistance.

"Please, Mommy," Sara cried. "We gots to do something."

A tear slid down Madelyn's cheek. The day the twins had been born was the happiest and saddest day of her life. She'd gotten Sara but lost her sister.

She'd heard that twins had a special connection, but why was Sara still dreaming that Cissy had survived?

Knowing neither she nor Sara would sleep well the rest of the night, she carried Sara to her bed, then snuggled beside her. Sara lay on her side, sniffling for another hour, then finally drifted into an exhausted sleep.

Madelyn's heart wrenched, and she lay and watched her daughter, unable to sleep. Just as dawn streaked the sky, her telephone jangled.

Who could be calling at this hour? She checked the caller ID. Her mother.

She grabbed the handset, then slid from the bed, walked to the window and connected the call.

"Mom? What's wrong? Are you all right?"

"Yes, honey, I'm fine. Have you seen the news?"

"No, why? What's going on?"

"A big story aired about a doctor in Sanctuary who stole babies and sold them. His name was Dr. Emery. Isn't that the doctor who delivered the twins?"

"Yes. Oh, my god. What else did the story say?"

"This lady named Nina Nash thought her baby died in that big, hospital fire eight years ago but discovered her child was alive. She hired these detectives at an agency called Guardian Angel Investigations there in Sanctuary. These men are all dedicated to finding missing children and they found her little girl."

A cold chill swept up Madelyn's spine. She glanced back at the bed where Sara was sleeping.

Dear God.

Was it possible that Cissy could have survived?

CALEB WALKER ENTERED the offices of GAI, his neck knotted with nerves. He hadn't liked the sound of his boss's voice when he called. The urgency had him postponing his visit to the cemetery to visit his wife's grave this morning, and that pissed him off. He'd wanted to go by first thing, to pay his respects, leave Mara's flowers, talk to her and beg her forgiveness one more time....

Gage's voice rose from his office, breaking into his thoughts, and Caleb forced himself to focus. There would be time for seeing Mara later. Time to drown his sorrows and guilt.

He climbed the steps to Gage's office, his mind racing. Had another child gone missing?

Or was there another case related to Sanctuary Hospital? Ever since the news had broken about the recovery of Nina Nash's daughter and Dr. Emery's arrest for selling babies, the phones had gone crazy.

People from all over were demanding to know if their adoptions were legal. GAI had been plagued by crank calls, as well, two from distraught women whose accusations of baby kidnapping had turned out to be false. The women had been so desperate for a child they'd tried to use the illegal adoptions to claim one for themselves.

Caleb twisted the hand-carved arrowhead around his neck to calm himself as he knocked on his boss's office door.

"Come in."

Caleb opened the door and Gage stood.

"I'm glad you're here," Gage said without pre-amble. "We have a new client. One I'd like for you to handle."

Caleb narrowed his eyes. "Why me?"

Gage's eyes darkened. "You'll know after you meet her and her five-year-old daughter, Sara. Sara insists she sees her twin in her nightmares, that her sister is in trouble."

"I don't understand," Caleb said. "Sounds like a child having bad dreams, not a missing person case."

"It gets even more interesting." Gage flicked his gaze to the conference room across the hall. "The mother claims the twin died at birth, but Sara insists she's alive."

Damn. Gage requested him because of his so-called sixth sense. He wished to hell he'd never divulged that detail.

But Gage had caught him in a weak mo-ment.

Gage motioned for him to follow. "Come on, they're waiting."

Caleb rolled his hands into fists, then forced

himself to flex them again, struggling to control his emotions. Emotions had no place in business. And business was his life now.

The moment Caleb entered the conference room, he spotted the woman sitting in a wing chair cradling the little girl in her lap. Gage had purposely designed the room with cozy seating nooks to put clients at ease.

But nothing about this woman appeared to be at ease.

Her slender body radiated with tension, her eyes looked haunted, her expression wary.

Yet he was also struck by her startling beauty. Copper-colored hair draped her shoulders and flowed like silk around a heart-shaped face. Big, green eyes gazed at him as if she desperately needed a friend, and freckles dotted her fair skin, making her look young and vulnerable. Her outfit was simple, too, not meant to be enticing—long denim skirt, peasant blouse—yet the soft colors made her look utterly feminine.

And downright earthy.

Earthy in his book meant sexy. Lethal combinations to a man who had been celibate for the past three years.

Dammit. He hadn't been attracted to another woman since Mara. He sure as hell didn't want to be attracted to a client. Not one with a kid who claimed to see her dead sister.

Then his gaze fell to the little blonde munchkin, and his lungs tightened. She looked tiny and frail and terrified and so lost that his protective instincts kicked in.

"Ms. Andrews," Gage began. "This is Caleb Walker. He's one of our agents at GAI. I'd like for him to hear your story."

The woman squared her shoulders as if anticipating a confrontation. She expected skepticism.

"You can call me Madelyn," she said in a husky voice that sounded as if it was laced with whiskey.

Gage claimed the love seat, leaving the other wing chair nearest Madelyn for him. Caleb lowered himself into it, aware his size might intimidate the little girl.

"What's your name?" he asked in a gentle tone.

Eyes that mirrored her mother's stared up at him as if she was trying to decide if he was friend or foe. Smart kid. She should be wary of strangers.

He smiled slowly, trying to ease her discomfort. But his senses prickled, suggesting she was special in some way. That she possessed a sixth sense herself.

Not that he would wish that on anyone, especially a kid.

"Let's see," he said, a smile quirking his mouth. "Are you Little Miss Sunshine?"

A tiny smile lit her eyes, and she relaxed slightly and loosened her grip on her blanket. "No, silly. I'm Sara."

"Hi, Sara," he said gruffly. "That's a pretty name."

"Thank you," she said, her tone sounding grown up for such a little bitty thing. "It's my Gran's middle name."

"Okay, Sara. Tell me what's going on so I can help you."

Madelyn stroked her daughter's hair. "Sara's been having nightmares for the past two months, ever since we moved back to town."

"Where are you from?" Caleb asked, probing for background information.

Madelyn hugged Sara closer. "We moved to Charlotte four years ago to be near my mom, but Sara was born in Sanctuary. Recently my mother suffered a stroke, and I found a nursing facility here that she liked, so I bought the craft shop in town, and we packed up and moved back."

"I see," Caleb said. Had the move triggered these nightmares? "Sara, did you have dreams of your sister when you lived in Charlotte?"

Sara nodded and twirled a strand of hair around her finger. "We talked and sang songs and told secrets."

Caleb narrowed his eyes. "What kinds of secrets?"

Sara pursed her mouth. "They're not secrets if I tell."

Hmm. She was loyal to her sister. But those secrets might be important.

"She has dreamed about her twin all her life," Madelyn confirmed. "But lately those dreams have been disturbing."

Sara piped up. "Her name is Cissy, and she looks just like me."

Caleb nodded, aware that she used the present tense. "Sara and Cissy. How old are you?"

"Five," Sara said and held up five fingers. "Cissy's five, too."

He smiled again. "You're identical twins?"

She swung her feet. "Yep, 'cept I gots a birth-mark on my right arm and hers is on the other side." She pointed to a small, pale, crescent-moon shape on her forearm.

Caleb folded his hands. He needed to keep

Sara talking. "Tell me what happens in your dreams, Sara."

Terror darkened the little girl's face. "Cissy is scared and she's screamin' and she runned into the woods."

Damn. He understood about nightmares, how real and haunting they could seem. "Who is she running from?" Caleb asked.

"From a big, mean man. He screamed at her mommy," Sara said with conviction. "Cissy says he's gonna kill them."

Caleb intentionally lowered his voice. "Can you see his face? Does she call him by name?"

Sara chewed on her thumb for a moment as if trying to picture the man in her mind. "No, I can't see him." Her voice rose with anxiety. "But I saw Cissy running and crying."

Caleb clenched his hands, listening, hating the terror in the little girl's voice. The last thing he wanted to do was traumatize a troubled child by doubting her or confirming her fears. And she was genuinely afraid and believed what she was telling him.

His sixth sense kicked in. This little girl was… different. Did she truly have a psychic connection to her twin?

Other questions bombarded him: If her sister

was dead, was Sara seeing and conversing with her spirit? Was Sara a medium? If so, why was she seeing images of Cissy at the same age as herself instead of the infant she'd been when she died? Was Cissy's growth a figment of Sara's imagination?

Another theory rattled through his head. Or could Sara be experiencing premonitions? Could Cissy's spirit be trying to warn Sara that Sara was in danger from some future attacker?

"You're a brave girl," Caleb said, then patted Sara's arm. "And if you see anything else—the man's face, or the mommy's—I want you to tell me. Okay?"

Sara bobbed her little head up and down, although she looked wrung out now, as if relaying her nightmare had drained her. Or maybe she was worried that describing the terrifying ordeal might make it come true.

He lifted his gaze to Madelyn. "Can we talk alone?"

Her wary gaze flew to his. "I don't like to leave Sara by herself."

Gage retrieved a pad of paper and some crayons and gestured to the coffee table. "It's okay, Madelyn. I have a little girl, too. Her name is Ruby and she likes to draw when she comes to the office." He stooped down and handed the crayons to Sara. "Would you like to use Ruby's crayons to draw a picture of Cissy while Caleb talks to your mother?"

Sara studied him for a long moment, then nodded. Madelyn reluctantly stood and settled Sara on the floor in front of the coffee table. Caleb gestured to the door, and she led the way out into the hallway.

The moment he closed the door, she whirled on him, arms crossed. "Listen, Mr. Walker, I know you probably think that Sara is disturbed, and believe me, I've taken her to shrinks, consulted with specialists, tried to talk to her myself, but these nightmares keep reoccurring, and there has to be a reason."

Caleb shifted. "Did these doctors make a diagnosis?"

Madelyn sighed, her expression strained. "Oh, yes, lots of them. The first doctor suggested Sara was seeing herself, that the twin was a mirror image. Doctor Number Two implied that she was terrified because she had no father, then suggested she made up the bizarre connection with Cissy to get attention. His colleague indicated Sara might be bipolar and wanted to put her in a special twin study, run a mountain of tests and analyze her brain." She blew out a breath, sending her bangs fluttering. "The last one suggested she was schizophrenic and advised me to let him prescribe drugs."

Caleb frowned. "Did you try medication?"

"No," Madelyn said emphatically. "She's only five years old." She paced across the hall, her hands knotting in the folds of her skirt. "I really hoped that I could handle it, that if I carried Sara to see Cissy's grave she'd accept that her sister is gone."

"What happened at the cemetery?" Caleb asked. "Did she see Cissy?"

Madelyn cleared her throat. "She insisted that Cissy wasn't buried in the grave. That it was empty."

Tears filled Madelyn's eyes, making Caleb's gut clench.

"But I know she is," Madelyn said in a haunted whisper. "Because I buried her myself."

Chapter Two

Sara's words haunted Madelyn as Caleb coaxed her into his office.

"Cissy's not dead, Mommy. She gots another mommy, and she likes to play dolls and read stories just like me." Then Sara had started to cry. *"But her mommy's in trouble and this mean man's gonna hurt her and Cissy."*

Only she *had* buried Cissy five years ago.

Caleb propped himself against the desk edge while she sank onto a chair.

"If you're so sure Sara is wrong, why did you come to GAI?" Caleb asked.

Madelyn desperately tried to decipher the intensity in his deep brown eyes. The man scared the hell out of her.

He was huge, broad-shouldered, muscular, dark-skinned, with shoulder-length thick, black hair, and had the gruffest voice she'd ever heard. His Native American roots ran deep and infused him with a quiet strength that radiated from his every pore but also made him appear dangerous, like a warrior from the past.

Yet he had been gentle with Sara and obviously the head of GAI trusted him.

"My mother phoned. She heard a news story about GAI uncovering some illegal adoptions associated with Dr. Emery, babies he delivered at Sanctuary Hospital."

"You delivered the twins there?"

"Yes."

"What about the father?" Caleb asked.

Madelyn chewed her bottom lip. "He left us when Sara started calling her dead sister's name. I haven't seen him or heard from him since."

Caleb frowned. "He doesn't send child support?"

"I didn't want it," Madelyn said. "Not that he would have come through. He was having financial problems back then, his business failing."

Caleb sighed. "I'm sorry. Tell me about the delivery."

Grief welled inside Madelyn. "The night I went into labor, I had a car accident," Madelyn began. "I was going to the store when a car sideswiped me. I lost control and careened into a ditch." She knotted her hands. "My water broke and I went into labor."

Caleb narrowed his eyes. "What happened to the driver?"

Anger surged through Madelyn at the reminder. "He left the scene."

Caleb's big body tensed. "He didn't stop to see if you were okay or call an ambulance?"

"No." Madelyn rubbed her hands up and down her arms. "And the police never caught him." Not that they'd looked very hard. And she hadn't seen the vehicle so she hadn't been able to give them a description of it or the driver.

Caleb's expression darkened. "So the accident triggered your labor?"

Madelyn nodded.

"Were you injured anywhere else?"

She shrugged. "Some bruises and contusions. I lost consciousness and the doctor said I was hemorrhaging, so he did an emergency C-section and took the babies."

Caleb's jaw clenched. "You weren't awake during the delivery?"

"No," Madelyn said, fidgeting.

"But you held the babies when you regained consciousness?"

"I was out for a couple of hours. When I came to, I got to hold Sara for a minute. She'd been in ICU, being monitored." Madelyn ran a hand through her hair. "But Cissy… No, I never held her. Dr. Emery said…she was deformed, still-born, that it was better that I not remember her that way."

Caleb arched a thick, black brow. "So you never actually saw your other baby?"

"No…" Emotions welled in her throat. She tried to steel herself against them, but memories of that night crashed around her. The fear, the disorientation, the joy, the loss… "I…was so distraught, so grief-stricken that the doctor sedated me." She wiped at a tear slipping down her cheek. "Besides I…I believed Dr. Emery. Then there was Sara, and she was so beautiful and tiny, and I was so glad she'd survived. And she needed me…."

Caleb's silence made her rethink that night, and questions nagged at her. If she hadn't seen Cissy, maybe she hadn't died or been deformed at all.

"Did the medical examiner perform an autopsy on the baby?" Caleb asked.

"No." Tears burned the backs of her eyelids. "I…didn't want it. Didn't want to put her through it."

Although maybe she should have insisted. Then she'd have proof that her baby hadn't survived, and she'd know exactly what had been wrong with her.

Sara's insistence that she saw Cissy in her visions taunted her. If Dr. Emery had lied to other people, perhaps he'd lied to her. "We have to talk to Dr. Emery and force him to tell me the truth about Cissy."

"I'm afraid that's impossible," Caleb said quietly. "Dr. Emery hanged himself the day after he was arrested."

A desolate feeling engulfed Madelyn. "If he's dead, how will we ever learn the truth?"

Caleb's intense gaze settled on her. "Trust me. We'll find the truth."

"Then you'll investigate?"

"Yes." He gestured toward the conference room and pushed open the door to where Sara was drawing.

The childlike sketch showed Sara and her twin sister displaying their birthmarks. A second picture revealed a greenhouse full of sunflowers, and a tire swing hanging from a big tree in the yard.

Sara had also drawn an ugly, hairy, monster-like man with jagged teeth and pawlike hands. "That's the meanie gonna hurt Cissy and her mommy," Sara said.

She turned her big, green eyes toward Caleb. "Will you stop him, Mister?"

ANXIETY KNOTTED CALEB'S shoulders. How could he say no to this innocent little girl? She seemed so terrified.…

But if he promised to save her sister and this woman and failed, he wouldn't be able to live with himself. Not after failing Mara and his own son.

Hell, he was getting way ahead of himself. First, he had to determine if Cissy Andrews was actually alive.

The fact that Sara truly believed that she was real was obvious. But he couldn't dismiss the shrinks' theories, either. Not yet.

Gage glanced at the sketch, then at him as if silently asking his opinion.

He gave him a noncommittal look. "We need access to Emery's records."

"Afraid that's not going to happen," Gage said. "He destroyed them before he killed himself."

Damn. So they had no records, and he couldn't push a dead man for answers. His visions didn't work that way.

"What about the lawyer who handled the adoptions?" Caleb asked. "Wasn't his name Mansfield?"

"Yeah. The sheriff brought him in for questioning. He's facing charges, but his case is still pending, so he was released on bail."

"Then we look at his records," Caleb said.

"D.A. already confiscated them," Gage said. "And she's not sharing. Not with privacy issues and the legal and moral rights regarding adoptions."

Caleb stewed over that problem. They didn't work for the cops or have to follow the rules. If he knew where those records were, he'd find a way to search them.

But talking to Mansfield would be faster.

First, there was something else that had to be done. Something that would be painful for Madelyn. But a task that was necessary in order to verify whether or not that grave held a baby.

"Madelyn," he said in a voice low enough not to reach Sara's ears. "We need to exhume the casket you buried."

Grief flickered in her eyes as she glanced at Sara who was madly coloring another picture of her and Cissy. This time they were holding hands, dancing in the middle of a sea of sunflowers.

"All right," Madelyn said firmly. "If it'll help us learn the truth, then let's do it as soon as possible."

MADELYN PICTURED THE Lost Angels section at Sanctuary Gardens where they'd held

Cissy's memorial service in her mind and nausea flooded her. Still, with the questions Caleb had raised, Sara's nightmares, and the revelations about Dr. Emery, she wouldn't rest until she knew if Cissy was really buried in that grave.

Compassion darkened Caleb's eyes. "Okay. We'll get the ball rolling."

Madelyn nodded, gripping her emotions with a firm hand. For so long she had accepted that Cissy was dead that it was hard for her to wrap her mind around the fact that she might have survived. That she might be living somewhere with another family. That a physician would actually deceive his patients and sell their babies.

But the doctor's arrest was proof of the possibility, creating doubts, and she had to investigate or she would always wonder.

Sara ran to her, waving her drawing, her ponytail bobbing. "Look, Mommy, Cissy's gonna be so happy when we brings her home with us. She loves sunflowers. They're all around her."

"The sunflowers are beautiful," Madelyn said, her heart aching as worry knotted her insides. Was it true that twins were only half of a whole? What if they didn't find out Cissy was alive and bring her home? How would Sara take the news?

Would she be able to move on and finally be happy?

Sara tugged at Madelyn's hand. "We gots to hurry, Mommy."

Madelyn stroked Sara's hair away from her forehead. "Sweetheart, that's why we're here. Caleb—Mr. Walker—is going to investigate and find out why you're seeing these scary things."

Sara angled her face toward Caleb. "Thank you for 'vestigatin', Mister."

Madelyn smiled in spite of her turmoil because, after all, Sara was a charmer. Caleb knelt and extended his hand to Sara, and Madelyn couldn't help but notice how strong and calloused and tanned his fingers were, how masculine.

"I promise I'll do whatever I can to help you, Sara."

An odd look crossed Sara's face, then she took Caleb's hand and turned it over in her own small one and studied his palm as if she could see inside the man through his fingers. Madelyn noted the breadth of his palm against Sara's tiny one and thought that Sara might be frightened of him, but she seemed to immediately trust him.

In fact, neither one spoke for a moment. They

simply stared at each other, silent, assessing, as if sharing some private moment.

"You gots an Indian name?" Sara asked in a whisper.

Caleb nodded. "Firewalker."

Sara's eyes widened. "You walks on fire? Does it hurt?"

Caleb shook his head then pressed a hand to his chest. "No. Not if you hone in on your inner strength and power. On peace and faith."

Sara smiled. "I gots faith that you're gonna find Cissy."

A pained look crossed Caleb's face. "I will do my best, Sara," he said gruffly.

Madelyn's heart melted. Sara had not only missed her twin sister, but she'd missed having a father, as well. And she had been so caught up in raising her little girl, on being a single mother, surviving the loss of her husband and Cissy and making ends meet, that Madelyn hadn't once considered a personal relationship with a man.

Or finding a father for Sara.

She didn't need a man, she'd decided long ago. Sara had her, and she would be enough.

Only she wasn't enough. And now she needed this detective's help.

Her breath fluttered as he swung his gaze up

to her. His dark eyes sparkled with questions, yet she also sensed that she could trust him.

She hoped to hell that was true.

Sara dropped his hand and skipped to the door.

"Caleb, you'll let me know what you find." She didn't know if she could bear to be at the exhumation.

He nodded, then extended his hand to her this time. Wariness filled Madelyn, but she slid her hand into his. An odd sensation rippled through her at the feel of his rough, leathery skin against her own. It had been so long since she'd touched a man that her belly fluttered with awareness.

She pulled away immediately. She couldn't afford to indulge in a romantic flirtation. Finding out the truth about Cissy and ending these nightmares for Sara was all that mattered.

As soon as Madelyn left, Caleb set the wheels in motion for the exhumation.

"Sheriff Gray said he expects this won't be the last request for one," Gage said. "Damn Dr. Emery."

"Damn him for killing himself," Caleb said. "He should have to face every patient he deceived and make things right." Although there was no restitution, nothing that could make up for the loss of a child.

"The sheriff said workers will be meeting at the cemetery early in the morning for the exhumation. They want to make sure it's as private as possible," Gage said.

Caleb nodded. "I'll meet them there."

Yanking on his rawhide jacket, he headed outside. Time to pay his respects to Mara.

Wind battered his Jeep as he plowed across the mountain toward the Native American burial grounds. As he parked and climbed out, the sounds of ancient war drums and echoes of fallen friends bombarded him. Stones and wooden markers etched with family names stood in honor of loved ones, while handmade Native American beads and baskets decorated others, holding treasures.

Gripping a bouquet of lilies in one hand, he crossed the graveyard, grateful he'd managed to bring Mara here where her own parents were also buried. He paused at their markers, then stopped in front of Mara's, his heart heavy as he placed the flowers on her grave.

Today would have been Mara's twenty-eighth birthday. If she had lived.

And his son, if he'd been born, would have been two.

That hollowness he'd lived with since Mara's murder gnawed at him, and he traced a finger over Mara's name. His throat tightened as an image of what his son might have looked like materialized in his mind.

A toddler with chubby cheeks, thick, black hair, dark skin, and brown eyes like Mara's. His son would have been walking and climbing onto everything now.

But his little boy had never had a chance...

The icy cold of the winter wind seeped through him, adding to the chill he'd felt for the past three years. Three years of living alone. Of wondering why Mara and his unborn child had been taken instead of him.

Three years of living with the guilt.

Gritting his teeth, he stood, the vision of his son disappearing in the foggy haze. But Mara waited, an ethereal beauty in her traditional white wedding dress.

Although each day he sensed her fading. That her soul was preparing to move on. That she was waiting on something...something she needed from him...

For him to let her go? He wasn't sure that was possible. The guilt alone kept him coming back, kept him praying, kept him...prisoner.

Why couldn't it have been him instead of her?

Sara's insistence that her sister was still alive echoed in his mind. He understood the draw Sara felt, the difficulty in letting a loved one go. Did Sara suffer from survivor guilt as he did?

The sound of a flute echoed in the wind, and he closed his eyes, remembering their marriage ceremony. The traditional Love Flute playing, the fire ceremony with the golden glow illuminating Mara's beautiful face, the Rite of Seven Steps, the moment the traditional blue blanket had been removed from around them and the white one enfolded them, signifying their new ways of happiness and peace.

Yet that happiness and peace had been shattered a month later with bullets that had been meant for him. Mara had been struck instead and died in his place.

Hell. A fat lot of good his vision or gift, whatever the hell it was, had done him.

He hadn't foreseen Mara's death or he might have been able to stop it.

"What should I do, Mara? I don't want this gift, and I sure as hell don't want that little girl to have it."

But he had felt something kinetic pass between them when he'd touched Sara's tiny hand.

He'd seen the dark images in her mind. Felt the violence she felt.

And he'd witnessed a little girl identical to Sara running for her life, disappearing into the dark woods just as Sara had described....

What if Sara was right? What if her sister was alive and in trouble?

"I know I failed you," Caleb said in a pained voice. "I just pray I do not fail this little girl."

Madelyn's big, green eyes and frail smile flashed in his head, and a twinge of guilt assaulted him. He had also experienced a faint flicker of awareness when he'd touched Madelyn, a current of desire he hadn't felt since Mara.

But that was wrong. Mara had been his wife. He owed her his dedication. His life.

The wind suddenly whipped through the trees, hissing as it tossed dry leaves to the ground and sent them swirling across the cemetery. The scent of wilted roses filled the air, the sound of broken limbs snapping mingled with the echoes of the dead.

He waited, hoped, prayed he would hear Mara's voice one more time, but a bleak silence followed.

He turned and hurried back to his Jeep, started the engine and peeled from the parking lot. Tomorrow was the exhumation. It wouldn't be easy for Madelyn.

But nothing personal could or would happen between them.

Not ever.

NIGHTMARES OF MARA AND HIS son tormented Caleb all night. He woke drenched in sweat. No wonder he had connected with Madelyn and her daughter.

He and Madelyn had both lost a child.

A five-mile run and shower, then he grabbed a Thermos of coffee and jumped in his Jeep. But dread filled him as he drove across the mountain to Sanctuary Gardens. The sheriff's car was parked in the cemetery parking lot, a crew of men a few feet away preparing to exhume the body.

Anxiety needled him as he swerved in beside the patrol car, jammed his hands in the pockets of his jacket and strode toward the sheriff.

Sheriff Gray extended his hand. "You must be Caleb Walker?"

Caleb nodded. "Thanks for arranging this so quickly. You have the paperwork in order?"

Gray indicated the envelope in his hand. "Signature from Madelyn Andrews giving us permission. The license. And—" he gestured toward a tall, white-haired man with glasses wearing a lab coat "—Environmental Health Officer present, as required by law."

Caleb glanced at the E.H. Officer as he met up with the men designated to dig the grave. The transport service with the second coffin arrived and the driver stepped out, then crossed the graveyard to speak to the sheriff while two men from the funeral home erected a tent around the grave for privacy and to show respect for the grave while the exhumation took place.

Sheriff Gray introduced him to the medical examiner, Dr. Hal Rollo, who seemed pensive as he waited to do his job.

Caleb had witnessed a couple of exhumations before, but none for a child.

The thought made his stomach knot.

"You really believe there's truth to the woman's story?" Sheriff Gray asked. "I heard her kid is the one stirring things up, that she claims she sees her dead twin."

So much for keeping that part of the story under wraps to avoid skepticism. "I guess we'll know soon enough."

He followed Gray over to the Lost Angels corner of the cemetery, noting the wrought-iron gate protecting the resting place for the little souls. Ivory doves were perched above a bubbling fountain, and a statue of Jesus, hands folded in prayer as he looked toward the heavens, sat at the head of the plots as if guarding the angels below. Bright flowers, toy trucks, teddy bears, dolls and various other toys had been left as if to keep the children company, marking birthdays and holidays. His throat tightened at the sight. Two rows back, he spotted the marker for Cissy Andrews.

The plot had been well maintained, her marker adorned with plastic sunflowers. A small photo of Madelyn and Sara also sat at the head as if to reassure Cissy she wasn't forgotten or alone.

Drawn to the spot, he walked over and knelt beside it, his vision blurring as he studied Cissy's name and birth date. Sometimes touching objects, items of clothing, people triggered his visions.

His hands shook as he reached out to press them over the small grave. Behind him the other men's voices faded to a distant hum. He hesitated, a sliver of apprehension needling him. He might see nothing.

Or he might see the child's small body in the ground.

Sucking in a sharp breath, he told himself he had to do this.

Reality slipped away and the wind screamed through the trees as he laid his hand on the mound.

Chapter Three

Madelyn's emotions pinged back and forth as she drove Sara to her mother's home. She had already called her assistant at the craft shop and asked her to cover for her for a few days. She needed time to see this through, and Sara needed her.

She so did not want to see Cissy's grave upturned. Or her body desecrated.

But she'd trusted Dr. Emery and the hospital staff, virtual strangers, with her daughter before, because of her vulnerable emotional state, and she refused to do that now.

She had to know for sure if Cissy was buried and, if not, where she was.

The images Sara had painted tormented her.

Please dear God, if she did survive, let her be okay.

She glanced at Sara who gripped her blanket in one hand, a bouquet of sunflowers in her other for her grandmother. Sara never visited without a bouquet, and she always insisted they were from her and Cissy, not just her. Why was Sara obsessed with sunflowers?

Could her daughter possibly have some kind of psychic ability? Madelyn had never actually believed in anything supernatural, but what if she was wrong?

Perspiration trickled down the back of her neck, and she gripped the steering wheel tighter, mentally giving herself a pep talk as she had over the years.

She could do this. She was strong.

She had Sara, and no matter what happened, nothing was going to change that.

"Mommy, I liked Mr. Firewalker."

Madelyn smiled, ignoring the tickle in her belly that the mere mention of the man's name evoked. "I think he liked you, too, sweet pea." She tousled Sara's hair, well aware that Sara didn't always make friends easily. Some of the children in preschool shied away when she boasted about a sister they couldn't see. "After all, how could he not? You're adorable and smart and have that gorgeous smile."

Sara beamed a gap-toothed grin, and Madelyn steered the station wagon into the driveway at the assisted living facility, Sanctuary Seniors, and parked in front of her mother's unit. A few months ago, her mother had suffered a stroke and was partially paralyzed on one side, leaving her confined to a wheelchair. But her mind was quick and seeing Sara always lifted her spirits.

Sara bounded out of the car clutching the flowers in one hand, raced up to the door and banged on the front. "Gran, guess who's here," she sang. "We gots a surprise for you!"

A second later, Liz Cummings, one of the health care workers, greeted Sara with a big hug.

By the time Madelyn made it inside, Sara was already perched on her mother's lap in the wheelchair, talking in an animated voice about the big, dark-skinned Indian who could walk on fire, and Liz was putting the flowers in a vase on the window ledge so her mother could enjoy them.

Sara's mother arched a brow as Madelyn entered. "So is this young man handsome, dear?"

Madelyn blushed. Her mother never ceased to play matchmaker. So far, Madelyn had managed to avoid a real date with the men her mother had thrown in front of her.

"He's big, so biggg, Gran." Sara threw up her hands indicating that he was gigantic, and

Madelyn bit back a laugh. "And he's gonna find Cissy. He promised."

Madelyn's smile faded. She hated to give Sara false hopes and then have her be even more devastated if things fell through. "Honey, he's investigating, but we can't be sure what we'll find."

"He will find her," Sara insisted stubbornly. "He said he would and he can walk on fire so he can do anything."

Madelyn's mother, Cora, stroked Sara's hair. "I'm sure he'll do his best, pumpkin. Now, why don't we have a tea party while your mommy does her errands? Liz brought us some cookies, but they look pretty bare to me."

Sara clapped her hands. "We can decorate them, Gran! We'll make 'em look like sunflowers for Cissy!"

"That sounds like a fabulous idea," her mother said.

"Come on," Liz said. "Help me put out the icing and sprinkles so we can make those cookies pretty."

Sara skipped to the kitchen with Liz but worry knitted Madelyn's brow.

"She'll be all right." Her mother wheeled her chair over and clasped Madelyn's hand. "And so will you."

Madelyn soaked in her mother's smile. She

loved her and Sara more than she could say. "I don't know what I'd do without you, Mom. Sara and I…we both need you."

Her mother barked a laugh. "Well, I'm not going anywhere, sugar. Now you go and do what you need to do. I'll take care of Sara while you look for Cissy." She tilted her head toward the sunflowers. "I think Sara is right. Cissy loves sunflowers."

Madelyn's stomach twisted. Apparently her mother trusted Sara's visions.

They exchanged concerned looks. But her mother refrained from commenting further on Sara's recent sunflower obsession. They'd both hoped it would play itself out, but now Madelyn wondered if the sunflowers might be some kind of clue to her other daughter.

Pasting on a brave face, she hugged her mother. "I'll call. You two have fun."

"We always do," her mother said with a beaming smile.

Madelyn's throat thickened, and she nodded, afraid if she spoke, the dam holding back her emotions would break, and she'd fall on the floor in a puddle and start sobbing. Once she started, she might not be able to stop.

The morning sun sliced through the bare trees as she jogged to the minivan, then drove around the mountain. Early morning shadows flickered across the dark asphalt as the sun fought through the storm clouds gathering above. She slowed as she spotted the cemetery, dread flooding her at the sight of the sheriff's car and the hearse.

The day of the funeral threatened to replay through Madelyn's head, but she hit the pause button in her brain and zapped it on hold. She refused to relive that day again now with all these men watching.

Swallowing back nerves, she parked and walked to the top of the hill overlooking the Lost Angels corner where the sheriff and three other men stood conferring. Where was Caleb?

Inhaling a breath to fortify her courage, she stumbled down the hill and through the iron gate. Sheriff Gray gave her a concerned look, but she rushed past them, then looked into the tent protecting the site.

Caleb *was* there, kneeling with his hand on Cissy's grave. His dark skin had drained of color, and an odd mixture of grief and pain marred his face.

What was he doing? Could he see inside the grave?

CALEB'S WORLD SHIMMERED out of control as he felt a vision coming on. Darkness pulled at him, dragging him into an endless tunnel, a pit of silence that stretched below the ground, desolate, screaming with secrets…

"Caleb?"

The sound of a woman's voice jerked him free of the spell.

"What are you doing?"

Twisting his head sideways, he spotted Madelyn staring at him, her arms crossed, her expression troubled.

He stood abruptly, taking a step back, confused by what he'd seen. By what he hadn't seen. He needed more time, dammit. And he wasn't ready to share his gift just yet. "Nothing. Just thinking about the case." He crooked a thumb toward the sheriff. "Are you ready?"

"Yes." Sheriff Gray gestured toward the E.H. Officer. "Madelyn, this is Oliver Gordon, the Environmental Health Officer. He'll oversee the exhumation."

Madelyn nodded in greeting, obviously struggling with the reality of the task to come and its ramifications.

Gordon cleared his throat. "For health reasons, I have to ask everyone to wait a safe distance away. We must respect this grave as well as the surrounding ones."

"Of course." Madelyn folded her arms around

her waist as if to hold herself together while the funeral home employees approached with shovels. The distress on her face made Caleb's protective instincts surge. He wished he could spare her this ordeal, but this exhumation was vital to whether or not they moved forward with an investigation.

Amanda Peterson, GAI's resident forensic anthropologist, climbed from a sporty gray sedan at the top of the hill and walked toward them.

Caleb gestured to Madelyn. "Come on, let's take a walk."

Her face paled, but she didn't argue. Instead, she allowed him to guide her up the hill. Fine tremors rippled through her body as she stopped beneath a giant oak. Caleb rubbed a hand along her neck, hoping to calm her.

Amanda approached them, her expression sympathetic. "You must be Madelyn Andrews." She extended her hand. "I'm Amanda Peterson. I work with Caleb and Gage at GAI."

"It's nice to meet you," Madelyn said. "I didn't realize another agent would be present."

Caleb's gut pinched. "Amanda is a forensics anthropologist. We thought she might be helpful today."

Madelyn's eyes widened as the implications registered.

"She's going to oversee the medical examiner's work," Caleb continued, "just so we can verify the findings. In light of Dr. Emery's lies, we can't be too careful."

Amanda tugged her all-weather coat around her. "I'm sorry, Madelyn. I know this is difficult."

"Yes, well, thank you for being here. If I'd had my wits about me five years ago, I would have demanded to see my child before I buried her."

"Don't blame yourself," Amanda said, her voice and smile genuinely understanding. "You were a victim. And we're going to find out just how much of one today."

Amanda's pep talk seemed to give Madelyn strength, because she offered her a tiny smile.

Amanda nudged his arm as she headed down the hill as if silently ordering him to stay with Madelyn. Hell, she didn't have to tell him that Madelyn was vulnerable.

But getting too close to her was dangerous for him.

"You didn't answer me earlier, Caleb," Madelyn said. "What were you doing at Cissy's grave?" Suspicion flared in her eyes. "Do you have some kind of psychic ability that you didn't mention? Is that why you believed Sara? Could you see inside the grave?"

Irritated that she'd caught him when he'd had no intention of revealing his personal visions, he hesitated. Telling her meant opening himself up to scrutiny.

His grandfather's image flashed in his mind. White Feather, a shaman, a man with strong faith and belief in the Cherokee customs, in the healing power of herbs and the earth. And in the healing power of love.

He'd also believed in Caleb, in his visions, because his grandfather simply believed that he was special.

But if he had been so damn special, why hadn't he foreseen the shooter that horrible day?

"Caleb, I'm not going to judge. I saw you with Sara, the look on your face. She trusted you and her trust doesn't come easily." Madelyn laid her palm against his cheek, stirring primal instincts and needs that had lain dormant too long. "Just tell me the truth," she said softly.

His gaze met hers, and something sweet and frightening and sensual rippled between them, a connection he'd never felt, not even with Mara.

Because he had never shared the truth about

himself with her. He had tried to be a man she'd approve of. A hard worker, a provider. They'd married because they both wanted to raise a family without the stigma of a mixed race.

But this sensual connection, this drive to be near Madelyn, was foreign and disturbing and heated his blood.

Arousing him.

Arousal and lust had no place in an investigation.

Self-loathing filled him. They were at a graveyard, for God's sake. And Madelyn was inquiring about his gift and how it might impact this case. Not because she was remotely interested in him personally.

"Sometimes I sense things," he said quietly, watching her for a reaction. "It's not an ability I can control or call upon at will. It just… happens."

Her expression softened. "That's the reason you believed Sara? You sensed something when you shook her hand?"

"Yes, I believe that Sara is special," he said by way of an answer. He jammed his hands in his pockets, ignoring the whistle of the wind bringing cries of the dead from the graves. He had to focus on one case here and that was the

Andrews child. The other lost spirits would have to find another medium to hear their pleas.

Madelyn shivered and rubbed her hands up and down her arms. Leaves fluttered down from the trees, scattering amongst the markers, adding bold reds, yellows, and oranges to the brittle, brown grass.

Madelyn cleared her throat as if summoning courage. "What did you see when you touched the grave?"

His former vision flashed back. But he wasn't certain it was a vision at all. A world of darkness spun around him, that long empty pit clawing at him.

Madelyn clutched his arm. "Caleb, tell me the truth. Please."

"I didn't see anything," he said gruffly. "It was just dark and…I felt an emptiness. I…can't explain it. Sometimes my senses, my visions aren't correct. Sometimes they don't even make sense."

The heartbeat of silence while Madelyn stared at him felt like an eternity. "Just don't lie to me," she said. "I may seem like a fragile woman to you, but I can handle whatever happens."

Caleb's hearing suddenly seemed more acute. He could hear the scene behind him, the voices of the sheriff and funeral workers. Twigs snapped in the wind, leaves rustled, the shovel crunched dry dirt....

"How long has Sara had these nightmares about Cissy?" he asked.

Madelyn sighed, the weary sound of a worried mother. "I told you, the past two months, ever since we moved back to Sanctuary."

"But you said she talked about her twin before?"

Madelyn nodded. "At eighteen months, she started acting as if she was playing with her. Even now, when she has tea parties, she sets a place for Cissy. When she colors, she draws Cissy and those sunflowers. When she plays on the seesaw, Cissy is always on the other end."

Her voice broke, and she pressed a hand to her mouth to regain control, then forged ahead as if she needed to share her story. "When she was a baby, she'd lay on her side and giggle and reach out as if someone was there."

Caleb's mind raced to paranormal research he'd done. "Parapsychologists believe that children can see ghosts when they're babies. They have a connection then, but once their innocence is lost and society trains them, they no longer believe, so the spirits don't appear to them anymore."

Madelyn chewed her bottom lip. "I read that,

too. But Sara never lost that ability. In fact, her connection only seemed to grow stronger. Last year she started insisting that Cissy was alive, telling me stories about things she did, places she went. That's when I got really worried."

Caleb heard the pain in her voice. "When you consulted the shrinks?"

"Yes." The wind swept Madelyn's hair into her face, and she tucked it back with her fingers. "Sara seems so certain that her dreams are real, that her sister is alive, that I started to believe her." Her shoulders fell. "Maybe because I really wanted to so badly."

"That's understandable." Caleb ached to touch her, to soothe the torment in her voice, but the only way to help Madelyn was to uncover the truth.

If Sara was right, then her sister had been kidnapped and adopted by another family, she might be in danger.... And if she was wrong, Sara's visions might be ESP—or she might have some form of mental illness.

Or she might be communing with a dead girl....

A noise down the hill jarred him, and he jerked his head toward the gravesite. Sheriff Gray had stepped outside the tent and was motioning for him.

"Walker, we're ready," Gray shouted.

Madelyn's legs buckled, and he caught her around the waist. "Sit down on that bench by the fountain. Let me see what they found."

Too weak to argue, she nodded and allowed him to guide her to the bench. His heart climbed into his throat as he left her small form hunched inside her coat, shivering on that cold, stone slab.

But he squared his shoulders, determined to end the questions in her mind. It was the only way she and her daughter could find closure and move on.

Clenching his jaw, he raced down the hill and stepped inside the tent beside Amanda. The mood was somber, reverent, racked with tension and dread.

Slowly the E.H. Officer opened the casket.

Caleb braced himself but shock still ripped through him.

The casket was empty.

MADELYN TWISTED HER HANDS together, willing herself to remain calm as she waited. But every second that ticked by felt like someone was pulling out her fingernails one by one. The sound of a car motor drew her gaze back to the parking lot, and she saw an elderly man exit a sedan and hobble toward a grave near the church. Probably his wife's.

Poor man. How long had they been married before he'd lost her?

She'd thought she and Tim would grow old together, not that he would abandon her and Sara when they needed him most.

Bitterness threatened but she tamped it down. She'd long ago vowed not to indulge herself in that emotion for fear Sara would pick up on it.

She never wanted her daughter to know the truth about her father.

Voices carried in the wind, and she spotted Caleb walking toward her. Her lungs squeezed for air at his bleak expression. A bird chirped from a tree nearby, and leaves fluttered down into the fountain. One landed on the wings of the angel, another at her feet.

She gripped her hands together, waiting, watching for the small casket to appear.

"Madelyn," he said in a gruff voice. "I'm sorry."

She lunged to her feet. "What's wrong?" Her voice cracked, and for the first time, she realized that she'd actually held out hope that Sara might be right. That Cissy was alive.

Suddenly oblivious to her surroundings,

she vaulted down the hill, stumbling blindly. Whatever he had seen, she had to know.

"Madelyn, wait!"

Her boots pounded the ground as she ran down the hill. All she could think of was seeing that tiny casket, knowing whether her daughter was in there…

Her pulse pounded, sweat slid down her temple, and she stumbled over a loose rock and felt herself flailing to remain on two feet.

Caleb caught her arm and righted her, then helped her to the tent. Her heart pounded as she stepped beneath the tarp.

Dear God…

She gaped at Caleb. "I don't understand," she whispered.

A muscle ticked in Caleb's jaw. "Someone lied to you, Madelyn. Dr. Emery, the funeral director maybe. But you didn't bury your daughter five years ago. You buried an empty casket."

Anger, shock and betrayal slammed into her along with a million questions. But the one fact that she latched onto was the one she wanted to believe more than anything.

The casket was empty because Sara was right.

Cissy was alive.

CISSY RAN AND HID BEHIND the door between the den and the kitchen clutching her dolly to her chest. They were screaming again. They'd been at it for a long time now.

"How could you do this?" her mama shouted. "Why?"

"Because you wanted a kid, you were grieving over losing Doug."

"I know, but you lied to me."

"Just keep your mouth shut!" the big man yelled.

Cissy peered around the corner and saw her mama reach for the phone. "It's not right," her mama cried. "What you've done… It's not right. No wonder Cissy has bad dreams."

"That kid is crazy. She always has been." He grabbed her mama's shoulders and shook her. "Listen to me. You call, you'll lose her, and I'll go to jail. You wouldn't do that to your own family, would you?"

"But Cissy has a right to know the truth," her mama argued. "And I won't go to jail because I'll tell the truth."

"The truth. Hell, you don't even know the truth, you stupid bitch." He slapped her mother across the face. "You're up to your damn eyeballs in this. The kid is evidence, and we can't leave evidence behind."

"What are you talking about?" Cissy's mama looked terrified as she leaned against the sink.

Terror streaked through Cissy, and she backed into the hallway, but she tripped over a pair of work boots and yelped. He heard the noise and swung around. His face was red, his nostrils wide. His eyes bulged like a madman's.

He was going to kill her.

"Damn kid," he mumbled then turned and stomped toward Cissy, his big footsteps pounding the floor like a giant's.

"No, I won't let you hurt my baby." Her mama grabbed his arm to stop him, but he swung his arm back with such force that he slung her to the floor. Her mama hit her head on the table with a whack and blood spurted and ran down her face.

Cissy bit back a scream. Tears blurred her vision.

His growl dragged her from her stupor though, and she turned and darted out the back door. The porch door slammed behind her. His loud bellow followed.

"Get back here, kid. Come on, we'll play a little game."

He didn't want to play games, Cissy thought, as she barreled down the steps. He'd hurt her mama and now he was gonna hurt her.

She had to get away.

She dashed down the steps as quick as she could and ran toward the greenhouse and the sunflowers. It was the only place she'd be safe.

Sweat streamed down her face, and she heaved for a breath as she shoved open the heavy door and sneaked inside. She tucked her doll beneath her arm, then pushed with all her might to shut the door, pulling the metal latch. Then she ducked between the rows of sunflowers, weaving her way until she was hidden deep within the rows.

Crouching as low as she could, she hugged her dolly to her, closed her eyes and felt the tears flow.

"Please, Sara, help me," she whispered. "I don't know how much longer I can hide."

The door rattled as he shook it. "Get out here right now, kid!"

Cissy rocked herself back and forth and rolled into a tiny ball. She could see her sister in her mind. She wasn't crazy like the big meanie said.

"Sara, please come and get me," she whispered. "I'm scared. I don't wanna die."

Chapter Four

Caleb contemplated the implications of the empty grave. He wished like hell Dr. Emery was alive to explain how he could have deceived Madelyn. She was a new mother, had been in labor, suffering from an accident, and he had lied to her about one of her babies. The enormity of that cruelty boggled his mind.

"I can't believe it…" Madelyn murmured. "After all these years of thinking Cissy was gone…of visiting her grave…"

A mixture of grief, shock, rage and desolation spread across her face, and he couldn't resist. He slid an arm around her to support her, wanting to offer comfort. She surprised him by bowing her head and resting it against his chest.

"She could be alive," Madelyn whispered in a tormented voice. "All this time, she could have been out there, alone, hurting, wondering why her mother didn't want her."

Caleb hated to remind her of Dr. Emery's

crimes and the other possibilities, but it was inevitable. And she had asked him to be honest.

"Or he could have given her to another family, Madelyn. A couple who wanted a baby and had no idea that Emery was stealing children from unsuspecting mothers." He paused. "A couple who loved her."

Her silent words echoed in his head even though she didn't speak them. *But she should have been with her mother and her twin.*

Madelyn furrowed her brows. "Except that's not what Sara saw."

He shrugged. "It still could be possible."

Pain flashed in her eyes again. "But if Sara was right about Cissy being alive, then maybe she's right about Cissy being in trouble now." She clutched his arms. "Caleb, we have to find her. Sara says she's in danger and so is her m—the woman who adopted her. We have to hurry."

The E.H. Officer, Sheriff Gray, the men from the funeral home and the medical examiner all filed from the tent.

"What the hell is going on?" one of the funeral workers muttered.

"The fact that there is no body proves Dr. Emery lied to Madelyn," Caleb said, "and that her baby might have been adopted just as little Peyton Nash was."

"But I thought that was an isolated incident," the medical examiner said, "that it was personal. The girlfriend of the baby's father and his mother kidnapped that little girl and arranged the adoption."

"Emery was guilty of more than that," Sheriff Gray said. "According to the files from the former sheriff, he had a problem with single mothers and liked money."

"But I wasn't single at the time," Madelyn pointed out.

Caleb considered that. "Maybe not. But you had two babies, and he was in the business. He probably figured he could take one, and you still had the other baby, so you wouldn't question him."

Madelyn clenched her jaw. "And he was right. But I haven't been okay and neither has Sara."

Questions ticked through Caleb's mind. "Madelyn's baby did not have an autopsy. Did you know Dr. Emery at the time, Dr. Rollo?"

Dr. Rollo wrinkled his brow. "No, I only came on last year. But I'm surprised the M.E. at the time didn't request one."

"Where is he now?" Madelyn asked.

"He died last year," Dr. Rollo said. "Had an embolism."

Dammit. Dr. Emery was dead and so was the

former medical examiner. "I want to talk to that lawyer, now."

Caleb firmly set his jaw. Jameson Stanford Mansfield. According to Gage, Mansfield was a sleaze.

If he knew anything about Madelyn's missing child, he'd find out. No matter what it took.

MADELYN PHONED HER MOTHER while Caleb studied the grave site and casket. He was examining the site to verify that it hadn't been disturbed by anyone prior to them.

"Yes, Mom, it was empty," she said softly.

"Oh, my God. So little Sara's visions are real?"

Madelyn's chest ached. How many times had her daughter tried to convince her that Cissy was alive, yet she hadn't believed her? "Yes. Maybe. Poor Sara, I should have listened to her before. She kept insisting Cissy wasn't in that cemetery."

Her mother's breath wheezed out. "You know your grandmother had visions."

"What?" This was the first she'd ever heard of it. "Why didn't you ever tell me, Mother?"

A labored sigh echoed back. "Because she didn't like to talk about them, said people thought she was odd because of them." Another wheezed breath. "All this time I hoped…prayed…Sara didn't have them. Although at the same time, I hoped she did."

Madelyn didn't know what to make of that. "How is Sara now?"

"She's okay at the moment, but she became agitated earlier."

"What happened?"

"She and I were drawing. She drew more sunflowers except this time Cissy was hiding in the midst of them."

A cold wave of fear washed over Madelyn. "I planned to go with Caleb to confront the lawyer who arranged adoptions with Dr. Emery, but I can come and pick her up right now."

"No, she's settled down now, honey, and she and Liz are decorating the cookies. Take your time. The sooner you find Cissy, the sooner these disturbing images and nightmares will end for Sara."

"Are you sure you're feeling up to it, Mom? You've had a difficult year."

"Oh, honey," her mother said. "Sara keeps me young. Besides, just knowing Cissy might be out there is enough to make me work harder to free myself of this wheelchair."

Tears threatened to surface. It would be a miracle if her mother walked again. And another one if she found Cissy and brought her home.

Both seemed light-years away and impossible.

She closed her eyes and sighed, hating that Sara was suffering. And what about Cissy? What was happening to her?

"Sara's calling me to help with the sprinkles." Her mother lowered her voice. "Be careful, honey. When Nina Nash tried to find her child, someone tried to kill her. And if Sara is right about a man threatening her and her adopted mother, going after them could be dangerous."

Chills skated up Madelyn's spine, but she shook off the fear. Nothing was going to stop her now. "I'll be fine, Mom. I'm with Caleb."

"Ahh, yes. That handsome Native American."

"Mother…"

"It's all right to lean on someone, Madelyn. Tim did a number on you, but not every man is a scumbag like him."

Her mother hung up and Madelyn shivered, then opened her eyes and looked across the graveyard. The small town was supposed to be a great place to raise a family, a haven for her and Sara.

But recently the revelations about the hospital fire eight years ago and now babies being sold made her wonder what other secrets lay in the town.

Did someone in Sanctuary know where her daughter was?

"SHERIFF, WE'RE GOING TO pay a visit to Mansfield," Caleb said.

Sheriff Gray shrugged. "Good luck. But don't expect a confession from the bastard. He's pleading innocence and lawyered-up."

"Maybe he'll talk to me," Madelyn said.

Gray studied her for a long moment. "It's worth a shot. But Mansfield is shrewd and devious. He also uses his money and his daddy's name to get his way."

"His money and name don't mean crap to me," Caleb muttered, already contemplating ways to force the man to spill the truth if Madelyn's pleas didn't work.

"But what about his records?" Caleb asked. "Is there any way we can look at those?"

Gray shook his head. "District attorney subpoenaed them. You can talk to her, but I doubt she'll share with the case pending. That and adoptions being sealed and the rights of the adopted parents being a priority makes these types of situations almost impossible."

Exactly what Gage had already told him.

Caleb ground his teeth. Then again, he didn't work for the cops or play by their rules. Wasn't that one advantage Gage had pointed out when he'd recruited him for GAI?

Madelyn glanced toward the empty casket. "What are you going to do with that coffin?"

"It appears to be clean." The medical examiner squinted through the sun. "But I'd like a crime unit to process it. All right with you?"

Madelyn nodded.

Caleb placed his hand at the small of her back. "Let's go, Madelyn. I want to pay a surprise visit to Mansfield."

Determination settled on Madelyn's face. "Me, too. If he knows where Cissy is, he'd better tell us."

Caleb rubbed her back. If he didn't, court would be the least of Mansfield's problems.

Caleb walked her to her car, and they agreed to meet back at GAI headquarters. A few minutes later, Caleb led the way inside the agency to Gage's office.

"Amanda filled me in when she called." Gage frowned. "So Emery's adoption ring was bigger than just the Nash case."

"It appears that way," Caleb said.

"I'll talk to Sheila English, the D.A., and see if she'll give us any leads," Gage said. "I also phoned a buddy of mine at the Bureau. I'll let you know if he has any helpful information."

Caleb shifted on the balls of his feet. "Thanks. Since kidnapping is a federal case, we might need him."

Gage punched his intercom button and requested Benjamin Camp and Derrick McKinney come to his office. Five minutes later, Ben Camp, the computer expert, stood with them, arms crossed and solemn as Caleb caught him up on the case. Derrick listened silently as well, his hands jammed in his pockets.

"The sheriff said Mansfield's records have been subpoenaed. It's going to be hell getting access to them," Caleb said.

Ben shrugged, a mischievous smile tugging at his mouth. "I'll see what I can do."

Derrick cleared his throat. "Madelyn, my wife, Brianna, has connections with several adoption agencies and the local orphanage. I'll have her put out some feelers."

"Thank you." Madelyn offered him a tentative smile. "I really appreciate all of your help."

Ben gestured toward Caleb. "Can I see you for a minute? My office."

Caleb nodded. "Wait for me outside, Madelyn."

She gave him a questioning look but did as he said. Caleb followed Ben to his office, curious.

He'd heard Ben had been in trouble with the law before, that his expertise had landed him in jail. But he didn't give a damn. "What is it? Did you find something already?"

Ben shook his head, reached inside his desk and slid a small device into Caleb's hand. "It's a bug. Plant it in Mansfield's office."

It was illegal and inadmissible in court, but that was the advantage in working with a private agency. They'd get information any way they could get it.

Caleb tucked the bug in his pocket. "Thanks, Camp. Oh, and see what you can dig up on Madelyn's ex. Tim Andrews."

"You think he's involved?"

Caleb shrugged. "Who knows? But the jerk left when Sara started calling her dead sister's name. That makes him suspect in my book."

"Sounds like a real winner," Ben muttered. "I'll get on it right away and keep you posted."

Caleb hurried outside and found Madelyn tapping her foot by his Jeep. "What was that about?"

Caleb shrugged and opened the Jeep door. "Just business."

Madelyn caught his arm. "Please, Caleb, tell me the truth. Do you know something about Cissy you're not telling me?"

Caleb covered her hand with his. "No, just speaking to Ben about research."

Her eyes flickered with unease, then trust, making his insides knot. God help him. He didn't want to disappoint her.

Her fingers curled beneath his, her skin soft, her hand small in his. The urge to hold her seized him.

Sensations zinged through him, heating his blood. His mouth watered for hers.

Suddenly the wind whipped her hair around her face, and a drop of rain pinged on the sidewalk. Madelyn clamped her teeth over her bottom lip as she glanced at the mountains.

The fear that stretched across her face jerked him out of his lust-driven stupor, reminding him that a little girl might be out there somewhere in danger.

No time for play. They had work to do.

"Let's go meet Mansfield, Madelyn. Maybe we can convince him to talk and get some answers."

MADELYN CLENCHED HER HANDS in her lap, missing the sweet comfort of her hand cradled inside Caleb's. For a brief moment, she'd felt a frisson of sensual heat rippling between them. But it must have been her imagination.

Caleb was a professional and had only been offering support in a trying time. She could not become dependant on him.

As he drove to Mansfield's office, images of Cissy flashed through her head. Where had she been all these years? Who was raising her? What kind of life had she had? Did she live in North Carolina? Near Sanctuary?

Was she loved?

Did she know that she had a twin or that she was adopted? What had her family told her?

Anger boiled inside her, as well, as picture after picture of Sara and Cissy together surfaced. All the years they could have been together, played together, shared toys and secrets and laughter.

And to think, Sara would have gone without nightmares these past two months.

And if Sara was connected to Cissy, did the connection work both ways? Was Cissy calling out to Sara for help?

Or could Sara be wrong? Only seeing what she wanted to see; that Cissy wanted to be with them because Sara missed her?

She swallowed back tears. No. She would not doubt Sara again.

"Madelyn, if you want me to drive you home first, I can do this alone," Caleb offered as he pulled in front of the lawyer's office and parked. The building was an older, Georgian-style house that had been renovated into an office, but it looked well maintained. She'd heard that Mansfield had family money, and that he used it to throw his weight around.

But she wasn't afraid of the man. And if he'd earned any part of that money by selling babies, *her* baby, she'd make sure he rotted in jail.

"No." She interjected steel into her voice. "I want to see this man's face when we confront him."

Caleb's gaze locked with hers. "Good. I think he should have to face the people he wronged."

She reached for the door handle and climbed out, then followed Caleb up the steps to the office. Traffic crawled by the downtown area, the sound of tires skating over slushy, wet leaves echoing behind them.

Caleb entered without knocking and she followed him inside. A chunky bottled-blonde with a miniscule skirt and cleavage to spare beamed a smile up at Caleb.

"Hi, Mister, how can we help you?"

"We need to see Mansfield," Caleb said, ignoring her flirtatious smile. "It's urgent."

"Is this a legal matter?"

"I'd rather speak to Mansfield about it in private." Caleb strode toward the door. "Don't bother to get up. We'll let ourselves in."

The woman's expression morphed from solicitous to concerned in a nanosecond, and she rushed toward the lawyer's door, tottering on three-inch heels. But Caleb was already stalking in. Taking his cue, Madelyn elbowed her way past the receptionist.

"What the hell?" A balding man jumped to his feet behind a massive, cherry desk and glared at them. "Brenda, what's going on? I told you no one gets through."

"Don't blame her," Caleb said in a tone that brooked no argument. "No one, especially your receptionist, could stop us from being here, Mansfield."

Mansfield reached for his phone, his scalp reddening. "I'm calling the police."

Their gazes locked in challenge. "Put down the phone," Caleb ordered.

Madelyn barely resisted the urge to pummel the man with her fists. "Tell me what you did with my daughter, Mr. Mansfield."

Mansfield's eyes widened in shock. "I don't know who you are or what you're talking about." He slanted a panicked look toward the doorway where his receptionist still stood. "Get my lawyer here now!"

Madelyn wasn't backing down. Instead, she leaned forward, planted her fists on his desk and gave him an icy look. "Don't pretend innocence, Mr. Mansfield. Just tell me who you sold my little girl to, because I want her back."

Chapter Five

Caleb narrowed his eyes, scrutinizing Mansfield, as panic etched lines across the lawyer's face. The creep was hiding something. He wasn't as innocent as he and his damn lawyer wanted everyone to believe.

"Tell me," Madelyn said sharply. "Where is my daughter?"

Mansfield shot his receptionist another frantic look indicating for her to hurry and make the phone call.

"You can call your lawyer," Caleb said sharply. "But we're not going away. We know you handled arrangements for Nina Nash's daughter's illegal adoption, and now we suspect that Mrs. Andrews's child was also abducted at birth."

"Like I said, I have no idea what you're talking about." Mansfield ran a shaky hand over his sweating forehead. "I don't even know who you are, Mrs. Andrews, much less anything about your child. And I don't recall seeing anything about a child abduction in the area regarding a baby named Andrews."

"That's because Dr. Emery lied and told me my little girl died at birth." Anger tinged Madelyn's voice. "He said she was deformed and it was better that I not see her."

Mansfield's nostrils flared. "Again, I have no knowledge of improprieties regarding you or your child. If Dr. Emery deceived you, then he did so without my knowledge."

Caleb cleared his throat. "Oh, come on, Mansfield. The D.A. has your files. She's going to fry your ass and you know it. So why not cooperate and help rectify the damage you did years ago by helping us find Madelyn's baby?" He hesitated, then continued, hoping to drive his point home. "Maybe the D.A. will even cut you a deal for your assistance."

"I did not sell babies!" Mansfield bellowed. "I'm an upstanding member of this town. Do you know who my father is?"

"I don't care if your old man owns all of the southern states combined," Caleb snapped. "All I care about is finding the child that was stolen from Madelyn Andrews."

Madelyn inched forward. "How could you and Dr. Emery allow me to believe that my little girl died? You all let me have a memorial service for her, watch that tiny casket be buried."

"I'm sorry for your loss," Mansfield said, desperately striving to turn on the charm. "But just because Nina Nash's baby was kidnapped—a kidnapping I swear I had no knowledge of—that doesn't mean your baby was, too."

"Mr. Mansfield, Dr. Emery delivered Mrs. Andrews's twins five years ago, and as she said, told her one of them died. But we just exhumed that casket and there is no baby inside."

Shock flared across Mansfield's face. "Even if he deceived her, you have no evidence that I had any part in it."

"You can check your files to see if you handled the baby's adoption," Caleb said.

"I don't have to check my files," Mansfield blurted. "I remember names and I did not arrange an adoption for any baby named Andrews."

"Her first name was Cissy," Madelyn said.

"As I said, I wasn't involved."

Caleb felt like choking the man. "You're lying and we're going to prove it."

Brenda tottered back in with a faint knock at the open door. "Excuse me. Mr. Mansfield, your father and lawyer are on their way."

"Thanks, Brenda." Mansfield swung his head

toward Madelyn, slightly calmer now he knew the cavalry was near.

"Please," Madelyn said in a pained voice. "I think my little girl is in danger. You can help us save her."

"I told you I don't know what you're talking about. All I did was handle paperwork for a few adoptions, but they were all legitimate."

"The Nash baby's wasn't," Caleb pointed out.

Mansfield's eyes bulged. "I was a victim the same as that mother! Now Emery killed himself, everyone wants to use me as a scapegoat!"

Caleb grunted sarcastically. "You are anything but a victim, Mansfield. You got paid well for your silence and now you're lying to cover your ass."

Anger reddened Mansfield's face. "You have no right to talk to me like that."

"Then prove you're telling the truth by showing me your records," Caleb pushed.

A vein throbbed in Mansfield's neck. "Even if I wanted to let you see them, I couldn't. There are confidentiality laws. I could lose my license as well as trust from clients and future clients."

"When I get through with you, you won't have any clients," Caleb growled.

A tense second passed as Mansfield fidgeted and glanced at the door, obviously searching for help.

"Please," Madelyn said softly. "I'm begging you. Cissy is in danger. Who adopted her?"

His face twisted with unease. "Any adoptions I arranged were between willing parties. Trust me, the adopted parents were desperate for babies."

"So desperate they didn't care where the child came from or if he or she was stolen," Caleb said bitterly. "Or how much money they had to pay to get the baby."

Mansfield's long-winded sigh punctuated the air. Footsteps clattered behind them, a door slammed, and another man's voice boomed as the man cleared the front office and stepped into the doorway.

"I'm Mansfield's lawyer, Leo Holbrook," a young man in an expensive, black suit said with authority. "What's going on here?"

"These people are harassing me," Mansfield said, his look flying to his father, an astute, gray-haired man with ice cubes for eyes, who appeared beside Holbrook.

"Mrs. Andrews just discovered that the baby she thought died five years ago may be alive," Caleb explained. "We thought Mr. Mansfield would do the right thing and help us determine what happened to her child."

"Mr. Mansfield knows nothing of this," Mansfield, Sr., said with a snarl. "Now get out before I sue you both for harassment."

Madelyn lifted her chin. "You don't frighten me, Mr. Mansfield. My daughter is alive, and she may be in danger. And I will do anything to find her." She stabbed a finger in his chest punctuating her point. "And nothing you or any of your lawyers do or say will stop me."

A small grin tugged at Caleb's face, admiration stirring in his gut as Madelyn squared her shoulders and brushed past the men leaving them stunned by her boldness.

MADELYN STORMED OUT TO Caleb's Jeep, furious and frustrated. "Well, that was a bust."

"Maybe. Maybe not."

"How can you say that? His lawyer and father are hovering around him like guard dogs. We'll never convince him to talk."

Caleb coaxed her into the Jeep, then settled inside the driver's seat. "Shh, Madelyn. There are other ways of finding out what someone is up to."

She crossed her arms. "How? He's not about

to admit anything. He's too worried about his precious career and money."

"True," Caleb said gruffly. "But trust me, Madelyn. I will do everything I can to discover the truth, to find Cissy." He took her hand in his and stroked it, and Madelyn felt like whimpering.

How long had it been since anyone except her mother had soothed her? She was the one who always comforted Sara.

But completely trust him?

She didn't know if she was capable of giving her complete trust to anyone. Not after the twins' father, the man who had vowed to love, honor and cherish her, the man she'd believed would love his children no matter what, had walked out on them.

She eased her hand from Caleb's, but her gaze remained fixed on his dark brown eyes. Eyes that could swallow a woman. Seduce her. Make her want to believe anything he said.

Dangerous eyes. Sexy eyes.

Eyes laden with promises.

Ones she didn't intend to fall prey to.

She wrestled her emotions into control. "What do we do now?"

Caleb drummed his fingers in thought. "Who assisted Dr. Emery in your delivery?"

Madelyn massaged her temple. She had relived that night so many times. Had berated herself for driving. Had blamed herself. If only she'd waited on Tim to go to the store, if she'd stayed home, if she hadn't been so hysterical when Dr. Emery had relayed the devastating news about Cissy…

The list of recriminations was endless.

"Madelyn?" Caleb asked.

"I'm sorry." She banished the guilt to that faraway corner in her mind in order to survive. After all, she had Sara, and Sara needed her. "I was unconscious," she said. "But there had to be some hospital staff on duty. Nurses. Assistants."

"Do you remember anyone specifically who talked to you about Cissy afterward? Anyone else who saw Cissy?"

Chills skated along Madelyn's spine. If Cissy had been born normal, if Dr. Emery had whisked her away to sell her, then someone else had to know. "My God. Dr. Emery had to have a helper."

Caleb arched a brow. "I'm going to ask Gage to track down the doctor who signed off on your baby's release to the funeral home. Which funeral home did you use?"

Madelyn frowned. "The one in Sanctuary. You think the director at the funeral home knew?"

"It's possible," Caleb said. "Think about the staff that night, the nurses. Anyone stand out?"

A shudder coursed through her. "I was so traumatized, it's a blur," she whispered. Images of faces, white coats, a man with glasses…a woman, heavy, short, curly brown hair, a gap between her front teeth…spun in and out of her head. "Come to think of it, there was a nurse, an older heavyset woman who tried to console me the next day. Her name was Nadine."

Caleb sped up. "Let's find Nadine and stop by the hospital. Maybe another employee remembers something."

Madelyn nodded, hope desperately budding to life in her chest. But if Nadine knew something, why hadn't she come forward sooner?

CALEB PUNCHED IN BEN's number. "It's Caleb. Have you found anything on those files?"

"Still working on it, but I'm getting close."

"How about Mansfield?"

"When you left, he and his father had words. His old man is irate that he's scandalizing the family name."

Caleb grunted his distaste. "Not that he was

involved in the phony adoptions, just that he got caught."

"Right." Ben made a sound of disgust. "Old Man Mansfield wants the case tied up and fast."

"Did Mansfield admit that he knew Emery kidnapped the Nash baby without the mother's permission?"

"No outright confession. His lawyer shut him up fast the moment he mentioned Emery."

Damn. "How about financials?"

"That gets interesting. Mansfield made size-able deposits over the past few years in both his personal and business accounts, some corresponding with the Nash baby's disappearance and Madelyn's daughter's, as well as a boatload more. According to the D.A., Mansfield admitted to professionally handling adoptions, but he insists he thought they were legit." Ben heaved a sigh. "I suppose it's possible that Emery passed on forged papers to Mansfield without his knowledge."

"Possible but unlikely," Caleb muttered.

"All the defense needs is to create reasonable doubt," Ben said darkly.

True. "But we're going to nail him." Caleb glanced at Madelyn, his chest clenching. "Will you have Amanda find out who signed the baby's release to the funeral home, and see if the same people are still running the business? If the director or one of his employees knew the coffin was empty, maybe we can force them to talk."

"Copy that," Ben said. "Maybe Mansfield will make a mistake, too, and we can catch him."

Caleb had started driving toward the hospital but had a second thought. "Listen, Ben, can you access Sanctuary's hospital records and find out if a nurse named Nadine currently works there? She was on duty the night Madelyn gave birth." He gave him the date and year. "I'd like a list of any staff working the E.R. or delivery as well, especially if they have a record."

"You don't ask much, do you?" Ben said sarcastically.

Caleb chuckled. "I have a feeling you can handle it, Camp."

This time Ben laughed. "I'll try to work my magic. Hang on and I'll search for the nurse."

"We should talk to the hospital director," Caleb said, thinking out loud.

"Doubt that will do you any good," Ben muttered. "He's denied any involvement in Emery's wrongdoings, and his lawyer has hired personal guards to protect him. The hospital is facing multiple charges in both criminal and civil court, and he's received threats and hate mail from anonymous sources."

Damn. Caleb heard the sound of keys clicking on the computer.

"Okay, I found Nadine. Last name is Cotter. She left the hospital and works for a private, home health care service." Ben paused. "Looks like she resigned a couple of months after the Andrews's twins were delivered."

Suspicious. "Do you have a home address?"

"One second." More keys clicked, then Ben came back. "Cotter lives at Widow's Peak just north of here." He recited the address. "And Caleb, I found something else."

"What?"

"Her bank records." Ben whistled. "Looks like Nadine came into some money about five years ago."

"How much?"

"Ten thousand," Ben said. "Could have been a payoff."

Caleb grunted. Ten thousand for her silence. For a baby's life.

Disgusting.

But that bribe had allowed Emery to go free so he could rob more women of their children and profit from it.

"We're on our way to Nadine's house," Caleb

said. "With Emery dead, maybe the threat of jail will convince her to talk."

THE SUN WAS STARTING TO set as Caleb and Madelyn drove up to Widow's Peak. Nadine Cotter lived at the top of a ridge surrounded by the Blue Ridge Mountains, miles from town or neighbors. Had Nadine turned into some kind of hermit, or was she hiding out from someone?

Madelyn studied the scenery. She liked her privacy, but she couldn't imagine living so far out that she wouldn't have contact with friends or neighbors. It was dangerous, too—black bears, coyotes and foxes roamed these mountains.

"What did your friend at GAI say?" Madelyn asked.

"Ben's still investigating."

"Did he have information about Nadine?"

A muscle ticked in Caleb's jaw.

"Tell me," Madelyn insisted. "I hired you for the truth, not to protect me from it."

His eyes darkened with concern and she realized the truth must be ugly.

"Caleb, please," she said, then touched his hand, immediately feeling a jolt connecting them.

His fingers tightened around the steering

wheel. "Nadine deposited ten thousand dollars a few days after you gave birth."

Madelyn gritted her teeth, blinking back tears as she turned to stare out the window. Ten thousand lousy dollars? Was that what her baby had been worth to the woman?

The winter chill suffused her, the brittle bare branches and brown leaves mirroring how empty and dead she felt inside. "I don't understand how a woman could do that to another woman," she said, haunted by the memory of crying in Nadine's arms. "For God's sake. She consoled me, she saw how grief-stricken I was."

"You'd be surprised at what people will do for money. Especially if they're desperate." He lowered his voice to a soothing pitch. "Maybe she had a good reason, Madelyn."

Bitterness shot through Madelyn. "There is no reason good enough to lie to a mother about her child or to steal her baby from her arms."

"I agree," Caleb said gently.

His compassion made her throat close, and she fought against breaking down. She had to remain strong, see this through, for her and for Sara.

And for Cissy. Especially for Cissy.

Gravel spewed from Caleb's Jeep as he sped up the drive. A faded yellow house with white shutters sat at the top of the hill surrounded by oaks and hickory trees. A cheap, metal carport had been erected beside the house to shelter the car, a rusted dark green sedan that looked as if it needed painting. A bird feeder that had seen better days was littered with dry leaves and twigs, its base tilting as if the ground was sucking it into the earth.

Caleb cut the engine and turned to her. "Do you want to wait here while I see if she's home?"

"No way," Madelyn said as she reached for the door handle. "I'm going to make her look me in the eye and tell me the truth."

Caleb clenched his jaw. "All right. But follow my lead."

Anxious to confront Nadine, Madelyn strode up the driveway to the porch, Caleb on her heels. Adrenaline surged through her as she knocked on the door. This woman might know where her other daughter was.

Then she could find her and bring her home. Sara's nightmares would end, and the twins would be together as they should have been all along.

There was no answer, so she knocked again while Caleb scanned the front yard. Several long seconds passed, her heart beating like a drum while she waited. But again silence.

Caleb frowned, then reached for the doorknob and turned it. Instead of being locked, the door screeched open. Surprised, Madelyn started to step inside, but Caleb caught her arm.

"Wait, let me go first."

An acrid odor permeated the air as she entered the foyer. The ticktock of an ancient grandfather clock punctuated the eerie silence. Caleb paused again, listening. "Something's wrong."

Madelyn's heart beat faster.

"Go back to the Jeep," he murmured.

"No, I'm staying with you." Madelyn latched onto his arm and trailed him as he peered into the connecting living room and kitchen. The room was dusty, filled with magazines and out-dated furniture, and dirty dishes were stacked in the sink, flies swarming.

Desk drawers stood open as if they'd been ransacked, the contents spilling out.

Had someone broken in? If so, what were they looking for? And where was Nadine?

A rumbling sounded from the furnace, old pipes groaning, and wind whistled through the eaves as Caleb moved to the staircase. He placed a palm on the rail, and his big body went still.

The sound of water pinging onto the floor

echoed from above, and the screech of a cat followed, shrill and nerve-racking.

Caleb inched up the stairs, and Madelyn stayed tucked close behind him until they reached the landing. A master bedroom sat to the right, the source of the water coming from somewhere beyond. A connecting bathroom?

Caleb halted, throwing out a hand to stop her, and she noticed the disarray in the bedroom. Clothes tossed from the dresser drawers, underwear dangling, cotton panties and bras dumped on a flowered chair in the corner. A jewelry cabinet plundered through, costume jewelry scattered across the carpet as if the intruder had been searching for something valuable, then had been furious when he hadn't found a treasure chest.

Judging from the outside of the house and the furniture, why would a burglar have thought Nadine had valuables?

The metallic scent of blood suddenly assaulted Madelyn, the foul odors of death swirling around her in a rush. Water dripped and pinged against the floor, then she spotted blood, a river of it streaking the worn, white linoleum in the bathroom.

"Dear God." Caleb spun around, gripped her

arms and tried to shield her from the sight with his body.

But Madelyn was frozen in horror, her gaze riveted to the floor where Nadine lay, her eyes staring blankly into space, her neck slashed, naked except for the towel wrapped around her.

A towel drenched in blood.

Chapter Six

Caleb silently murmured a Cherokee prayer at the sight of the dead woman. She'd been brutally assaulted and left naked lying in her own blood. Whoever had killed her was not only a cold-blooded killer, but he had no respect for women...or human life itself.

Madelyn gasped in horror, and he instinctively yanked her into his arms and backed her away from the bedroom into the hallway. He'd known something was wrong when he'd entered, had felt the violence in the house.

"Oh, my God," Madelyn whispered. "Nadine... she's been murdered."

"Don't touch anything, Madelyn."

Madelyn nodded, trembling. "I can't believe this. The poor woman. Who would do such a horrible thing?"

Caleb stilled, listening, his mind already ticking away possibilities. Judging from the signs of rigor and the bloodstains, Nadine had probably been dead for hours, maybe even a day or two.

"Why would someone come all the way out here to rob Nadine?" Madelyn frowned at the mess. "What were they looking for?"

Caleb's thoughts fast-tracked into detective mode. If the perp was a drug addict or homeless person, they might be looking for cash or anything to sell.

But the pervading presence of evil simmered in the tension-laden air. "This doesn't look like a burglary gone bad," Caleb said. "The degree of violence, the lack of hesitation wounds, the force and depth of the slice on the woman's throat indicates intent." And the timing definitely added to his suspicions. If Nadine had information about Cissy's abduction, someone could have killed her to keep her quiet.

Madelyn's pallor turned a dismal gray as the implications sank in. "You think it has to do with me? With us looking for her?" Hysteria tinged her voice. "How would anyone know we were coming here?"

"I don't know," Caleb said, ushering her down the stairs. Unless the killer learned Madelyn had hired a detective. It was a small town, and word had probably spread that they'd been asking questions. And if the exhumation itself had been leaked, the killer/abductor would realize they knew the grave was empty.

"Mansfield knew we were working together. He might have guessed our intentions and warned whoever else was involved," Caleb finally answered.

"So either Mansfield or another accomplice is trying to shut people up," Madelyn said, her tone tinged with disbelief.

"Right." The thought made fury rail through him. The conniving, lying bastard.

And even if Mansfield hadn't killed the woman himself, he could have hired cronies. A man like him—or his father—wouldn't bloody his own hands.

However, he might murder to protect himself from prison.

He coaxed Madelyn into the living room, scanning the outside of the house through the windows as he punched in Ben's number.

"GAI. Camp speaking."

"It's Walker. We're at Nadine Cotter's. She's dead." Caleb paced by the window, checking outside again as Madelyn sank into a chair. He could see the wheels turning in her head. She was probably thinking about Nadine, that she'd lost her chance to find out whatever information the woman possessed.

"What happened?" Ben asked.

"Someone slashed her throat. I need you to call the local sheriff and get him out here with a crime unit. But give me a few minutes. I'd like to look around first." Although if whoever had broken in was hunting for evidence Nadine had hidden about the adoptions, they might have already found it.

Still, he had to search himself.

"You got it," Ben said.

"And keep an ear out for Mansfield," Caleb added. "If he was behind this woman's murder, maybe he'll spill his guts and we can catch him."

THE IMAGE OF NADINE'S dead body was imprinted in Madelyn's brain. She had seen news reports of murders before but never anyone close and personal. All that blood...

And with Nadine gone, how would Madelyn know if she'd been involved in her daughter's disappearance?

What if she never found Cissy?

Accepting Cissy's death had been difficult enough, but she couldn't rest now, not knowing she was alive and possibly in danger.

Caleb disconnected the call, then shifted. "I'm

going to my car for gloves, then I'll search the house before the police arrive."

Madelyn shifted. "What are you looking for?"

Caleb shrugged. "Evidence that Nadine knew about the adoptions. Maybe someone sent her a threatening note. Or she could have kept a journal or date book."

Madelyn's gaze swung across the kitchen to the adjoining living room. The killer might have ransacked the house to cover his tracks.

Which meant that the killer was aware that Nadine knew about Emery's illicit dealings. But who?

The back door from the kitchen stood slightly ajar, and Caleb walked over and studied it. "The lock's been jimmied," Caleb said. "This is how the killer got in."

Madeline pulled herself together and removed her own gloves from her jacket pocket. Nadine's body needed to be tended to. Her family notified.

Guilt assaulted her for searching her private space.

But if Nadine had known about Cissy and kept silent all these years, then Madelyn shouldn't feel guilty.

Caleb clenched her arms. "Madelyn, let me do this. I don't want you involved."

Hysterical laughter bubbled in her throat. "I am involved, Caleb. If we both search, we can finish faster, then the police can come."

He stared at her for a heartbeat, then nodded in concession. "All right. But let me get some latex gloves for both of us. I'll take the upstairs and you check the kitchen and living room."

Madelyn's heart raced as he hurried outside to the Jeep. Seconds later, he returned and they both donned the gloves. "Put everything back like you found it," Caleb added. "We don't want to interfere with the investigation, just see if there's anything that can help us nail Mansfield or lead us to Cissy."

Madelyn agreed, then started with the kitchen desk and drawers while Caleb disappeared up the stairs. She found shopping receipts, coupons, thank-you notes from several patients' families, paycheck stubs from the medical service where Nadine was employed and insurance statements along with bills that hadn't been paid.

Frustrated when the kitchen turned up nothing, she moved to the den and examined the coffee table, the drawers in the end tables and the coat closet. Nothing there, either.

Footsteps sounded, and Caleb descended

the steps, his expression solemn. "Did you find anything?"

"No. How about you?"

He shook his head. "If she had a journal or received threats, the killer must have taken the evidence." His gaze fell to the fireplace, and he strode over and squatted down.

Using the fire poker, he dug through the ashes, unearthing the charred remains of a leather-bound book.

Madelyn's pulse pounded. "Is it salvage-able?"

Caleb lifted it to study the contents, but the pages disintegrated into ashes, scattering onto the hearth. A siren wailed in the distance, and Madelyn wanted to scream.

They had been too late for the evidence and too late for Nadine.

What were they going to do now?

CALEB POCKETED HIS AND Madelyn's gloves, then he and Madelyn stepped onto the front porch to meet the sheriff.

Sheriff Gray stepped from the squad car; a deputy emerged from the passenger side.

Sheriff Gray crooked his head toward the deputy. "This is Deputy Stone Alexander."

Caleb extended his hand. "Caleb Walker, GAI. This is Madelyn Andrews, my client."

"The sheriff filled me in about the exhumation," Deputy Stone said.

"What are you doing here?" Gray asked. "You found a body?"

Caleb nodded. "Mrs. Andrews and I drove out to talk to Nadine Cotter, the woman who lives here, about Mrs. Andrews's missing child."

"I remembered her from the hospital," Madelyn said. "She was on duty the night I delivered the twins."

"I see." Sheriff Gray made a sound in his throat. "Go upstairs, Alexander. Check out the scene. I'll be right up."

Deputy Alexander nodded and climbed the stairs, then Gray turned back to them. "So you broke into the house and found her dead?"

Madelyn started to speak, but Caleb cleared his throat, piping up first. The last thing he wanted was for Madelyn to implicate herself with a motive. "No. We knocked several times but when there was no answer, I tried the door. It swung open, and I noticed that the place was in disarray then smelled blood, so I came in to see if Nadine was all right."

Sheriff Gray gave them both a long, assessing stare.

"It looks like she might have been dead for a while," Caleb said before the sheriff could ask more questions. "Someone slashed her throat."

"Did either of you touch anything?"

Caleb shook his head. "No. But Madelyn was in shock, so I brought her downstairs to sit down."

The sheriff gave them another curious look as if he was trying to decide whether or not to believe them, then moved toward the front door. "Wait outside until the crime van arrives." He glared at Caleb. "You will wait, won't you?"

"Of course," Caleb said. "I'm a professional, Sheriff. All we want are answers."

The next two hours dragged by as the medical examiner arrived, and the sheriff and crime unit examined the scene.

"You were right," Dr. Rollo said after he'd completed his initial exam. "I'd put time of death sometime during the night or early this morning. Rigor's already setting in."

"My bet is on Mansfield," Caleb said. "He was pretty upset when we questioned him."

The sheriff cocked his head sideways. "You think he killed Miss Cotter to cover himself."

Caleb shrugged. "What better way to silence her than murder?"

MADELYN WRESTLED WITH GUILT as Caleb drove her to pick up her car at GAI.

"I'm going to phone Ben and see if he's made any headway hacking into that list."

"It's late. I need to pick up Sara." Madelyn jiggled her keys. "My mom adores her, but she needs her rest."

Caleb nodded. "I'll let you know if Ben finds anything."

The weight of the day washed over Madelyn. Cissy was alive.

But Nadine, her only lead, was dead. Murdered.

Perhaps because someone didn't want her to find Cissy.

Caleb squeezed her shoulder, and Madelyn had the insane urge to lean into him. To ask him to hold her and make her forget the image of Nadine's blood splattered all over the bathroom floor.

"Madelyn, it's not your fault, you know," Caleb said gruffly.

She jerked her gaze to his. "Isn't it?"

"No," Caleb said matter-of-factly. "If Nadine was killed because of her involvement in Cissy's disappearance, she was guilty of conspiracy and should have come forward."

"Maybe." Madelyn ached inside. "But what

if Emery or Mansfield, or whoever else was involved, coerced her into cooperating? Maybe they threatened her family or her. Then she was a victim, too."

"That's possible. But she could have turned to the police or someone else for help," Caleb suggested.

Madelyn's mind worked. "Maybe she'd decided to come forward."

"That's possible," Caleb agreed.

But they might never know. The secrets Nadine had hidden would be buried with her in her grave.

And what about Cissy? Did her adopted parents know she'd been stolen from her real mother? Was she in danger?

Would she ever find her now?

Her shoulders sagging from the stress of the day, she climbed in her minivan and started for her mom's. Caleb watched as she backed from the drive, and once again, she had the crazy urge to stop and ask him to go home with her. To hold her hand tonight.

To stay with her and help her forget.

But Madelyn had a daughter to think of. She had no time to think about herself.

One man had hurt her terribly and abandoned

her and their child. She wouldn't give another man the chance to break her heart.

Swinging the van around, she sped toward Sanctuary's seniors home, pushing thoughts of Caleb from her mind. He was a detective. A man she'd hired to help her.

That was all he would ever be.

The quiet of the small town reminded her that Sanctuary was supposed to be safe, but Madelyn felt the darkness smothering her like a storm cloud ready to unleash more misery on her soul.

The ten-minute drive passed in a blur, and she parked and rushed in to get Sara.

"We've had a great day." Her mother patted Sara where she lay curled on the sofa with her blanket asleep.

Madelyn hugged her mother. "Thanks for letting her stay so long."

"You don't have to thank me, honey. We're family." The corners of her eyes crinkled with worry. "Poor child was so exhausted she conked out about a half hour ago."

"She didn't sleep well last night," Madelyn admitted.

Madelyn's mother clutched her hand. "Did you make any progress?"

Madelyn flinched. "The lawyer who handled

the adoptions won't talk. And we went to see one of the nurses who was on staff the night I delivered, but she had been murdered."

"Oh, my God, that's horrible." Madelyn's mother squared her shoulders. "But you can't give up, honey. You will find Cissy and bring her home where she belongs."

The tears were threatening, but Madelyn blinked them back. "You're always so strong, Mom, so positive." She hugged her hard. "Thank you for giving me courage."

Her mother held her for a long moment, massaging her back like she had when Madelyn was little, and emotions nearly overwhelmed her. Three generations—her mother, her, Sara and Cissy—were all bound together in love and loyalty.

They all needed answers and closure to move on.

"I love you, Madelyn," her mother whispered. "But I won't be around forever. I want you to find someone, a good man for you, a father for the girls."

"Mom, hush, don't even talk like that." In spite of her best efforts, a tear slipped down Madelyn's cheek. "Sara and I love you with all our hearts. *You* are all we need. And one day soon I'll bring Sara and Cissy here to see you, and you're going to take a walk with us and everything will be all right again."

Her mother laughed softly. "Yes, darling, that is the picture I see, too."

Madelyn clung to her for a moment, then realized she needed to let her mother rest. So she blinked back her tears, kissed her mother on the cheek, then released her and scooped a sleepy Sara into her arms and carried her to the car.

Sara roused for a moment. "Mommy?"

"Yes, precious, I'm here." Madelyn kissed Sara's cheek then buckled her in and drove them home.

Her house seemed unusually quiet and lonely, she thought, as she carried Sara up the stairs and tucked her into the white twin bed.

Then haunted by the memory of Nadine's blood and too anxious to sleep, she descended the steps to make a cup of tea. Or maybe she'd break down and have a glass of wine.

But the phone trilled as she hit the bottom step. Thinking it might be her mother or her nurse, or Caleb, she rushed over and yanked up the handset. "Hello."

"Stop nosing around," a low coarse voice growled. "Or you'll lose Daughter Number Two this time."

Chapter Seven

Caleb rapped his knuckles on the glass windows of Camp's office door, mentally stewing over the fact that Nadine, their closest lead, had been murdered.

The bastard who'd slashed her throat had wanted to keep her quiet. Which meant he was scared.

Ben motioned him in, then leaned back in his chair. Caleb sensed he was wired and wondered what he'd discovered. "Sheriff met you at the Cotter house," Ben said.

Caleb nodded. "Forensics is processing the place now. I doubt they find anything though. Killer ransacked the house to make it look like a robbery. I found a journal that had been burned in the fireplace."

Ben chewed the inside of his cheek. "You must be on the right track."

Yeah, but not fast enough. "Can you examine Nadine Cotter's phone records?" Caleb asked.

"Maybe the killer has had contact with her the past few weeks…or months."

Ben began digging through computer printouts on his desk. He was like a mad scientist, scattered, but brilliant at his job. Even better, he covered his tracks so the cops and feds couldn't trace him.

"Madelyn said there were late bills in Nadine's kitchen," Caleb continued. "Maybe she went back for more blackmail money."

"And the killer got nervous and ended it."

Caleb's cell phone vibrated on his hip, and he reached for it to check the number just as Ben pushed the papers toward him.

"Here's a preliminary list of people who used Mansfield's services for adoptions."

"There were ten names I've found so far. Six babies were boys, so I ruled those out. Three couples lived in North Carolina. The fourth couple moved to Tennessee, although they've fallen off the radar. I'll keep searching for an address."

Caleb's phone vibrated again, and he punched the connect key. "Madelyn?"

"Caleb, I… A man just called and threatened me."

Caleb rushed down the stairs and outside. "What did he say?"

Madelyn's shaky breath echoed back.

"Madelyn? Is someone there?"

"No… At least not now." She sighed shakily. "But I'm scared, Caleb. He said if I didn't stop nosing around, that I'd lose D…Daughter Number Two."

Son of a bitch!

Caleb jumped in his Jeep. "Lock all the doors, Madelyn. I'll be right there."

YOU'LL LOSE DAUGHTER Number Two this time. Daughter Number Two…Daughter Number Two…

The taunting voice echoed over and over in Madelyn's head.

No! She ran to the kitchen and checked the lock on the back door, then raced from room to room checking the windows. Her heart pounded as she slipped into Sara's room and stood by her bed watching her sleep, soaking in the fact that for now she was safe and alive and in her own bed.

She clenched and unclenched her fists. No one would hurt Sara. They would have to kill her first.

She needed a gun. Some way to defend them. She'd ask Caleb to suggest the best place for her to buy one in the morning. There was no way she'd let anyone hurt Sara.

You'll lose Daughter Number Two this time...

Whoever this man was, he knew what had happened to Cissy.

Did he know where she was now?

Frantic, she raced back down the steps, grabbed the phone and checked the caller log for a number, but the display screen showed *Unknown*.

Coward. He was a coward who stole children and threatened mothers and didn't even leave his name.

She'd kill him if she ever found him. Kill him if he hurt Cissy....

A car engine sounded, rumbling as it beat a path up her drive. The wind howled off the mountain, whipping at the roof of the wooden house. Clenching the phone in one hand, she dashed to the window, flipped on the porch light and peered out.

Car lights fanned the front porch, then a Jeep screeched to a stop. Her breath puffed out in relief, and she started to run to the door but caution made her wait until she saw Caleb emerge from the SUV. His big body looked ominous in the moonlight, his long hair falling loose and brushing his collar, his expression dark as he scanned the yard and perimeter in search of a predator.

The threatening call taunted her again, and she flew to the door and swung it open. Caleb climbed the porch steps in three quick strides, his strong jaw snapped taut as he met her gaze.

"Are you all right?"

She shook her head no, then fell into his arms.

CALEB WRAPPED HIS ARMS around Madelyn and held her tight. His heart had nearly pounded out of his chest on the way over. He kept imagining that someone had been outside Madelyn's house, lurking in the bushes, waiting to attack.

Waiting to slash her throat just as he had Nadine Cotter's.

And then little Sara… Was this killer so evil that he would hurt a child?

Madelyn clung to him, and he stroked her back, rocking her gently. She felt so tiny in his arms, so fragile, and she had been through so much today already that he had to make her feel safe. "It's all right, Madelyn. I won't let him hurt you or Sara."

Even as he made the promise, recriminations

screamed in his head. He'd vowed to protect Mara, too, but he had lost her and his unborn son.

He couldn't fail this woman and her child, too.

"I can't believe this is happening," Madelyn said, then stared up at him, her big eyes swimming in shock. "I want a gun, Caleb," she said, that fierceness back in her tone. "I need protection for me and Sara."

Mixed feelings warred in Caleb's head. "Madelyn, I know you're scared, but I'm not sure a gun is the answer. Not with a child in the house."

"But you carry a weapon," she argued. "And I can't leave us vulnerable. I have to take action."

"You took action," he said in a soothing tone. "You hired me, and I promise to protect you and Sara and find the person who kidnapped Cissy."

"But you won't always be around," Madelyn said. "One day we'll be alone, and I need to know that I can keep my girls safe. They need to know it, too. They shouldn't have to grow up afraid all the time."

That picture disturbed Caleb, as well. He wanted to promise Madelyn he would be around forever, but that would be a lie. When the case ended, she'd move on with her life. Find some man worthy to be her husband and a father to her girls.

He admired Madeline's gutsy attitude. But considering shooting someone and actually following through were two different things. Too many times an intruder managed to wrestle the person's gun away and turn it against him.

Tormented by the desperation in her voice though, he spoke softly. "Listen, when there's time to teach you how to use a weapon safely, I'll teach you myself. It would probably be a good idea for you to take some self-defense classes, too. But for now, trust me."

He hoped to hell he wasn't asking for blind trust that he couldn't deliver.

Fear darkened her eyes, but he sensed he was getting through. "I guess I'm just panicking," she said in a hoarse whisper. "That man…the threat… His voice sounded so ominous."

"Which means we're on the right track and he's scared," Caleb said. A strand of hair fell across her cheek and he brushed it back. "It means Nadine's death must be related to our investigation, that she was hiding something."

"But she died and now we'll never find out what she knew," Madelyn said, her voice warbling.

"Not necessarily," Caleb said. "Ben is examining her phone records, so if the killer has been communicating with her, we can track him down. He's also cross-checking her calls with yours to see if there's a common number." He paused, arching a brow. "And if you'll agree, I'll have him place a trace on your phone so if this bastard calls back, we might be able to track his location."

Hope flickered in her eyes. "Of course you can trace my calls," she said. "Anything to protect Sara."

"Good." Caleb forced himself to release her. He liked the feel of her close to him too damn much. This was a case, and that was all it could be. He couldn't become attached to her or her child.

"Ben gave me a list of couples who used Mansfield to handle their adoptions," Caleb said. "There are four names we need to check out. They may not have Cissy, but it's a place to start."

Excitement lit her face. "Oh, my God, Mansfield disclosed his list?"

"Not exactly." Caleb shot her a warning look not to probe, then led her to the kitchen table and handed her the printout. "Study these names and see if any of them sound familiar."

She frowned as she read the names. "No one rings a bell. You think the person who adopted Cissy was someone I knew?" she asked in an incredulous tone.

"I don't know," Caleb said honestly. "The adopted parents could have been innocent, unaware that Cissy was kidnapped."

Anxiety replaced the hope in her expression. "That's true, but Cissy is my little girl. And if Sara says she's in trouble, I believe her." She jutted up her chin. "If you don't, Caleb, I need to find someone who does."

Caleb wanted to deny that he believed Sara's gift, but how could he when he was cursed with his own sixth sense? When he knew gifts like theirs couldn't be trusted, but they sure as hell couldn't be ignored, either?

Because if Sara was right about a man threatening Cissy and her mother, and this killer was panicked enough to kill Nadine to silence her, he might kill Cissy and her mother to cover his tracks.

"SHOULD I CALL SOMEONE else?" Madelyn asked.

Caleb shook his head. "No. I promised I'd find out what happened to your daughter, and I will. But there is something I need to ask you."

Madelyn stared at him warily. "What?"

"Is there anyone you can think of who would have wanted to hurt you years ago?"

Madelyn frowned. "No. Not that I know of."

"Did your family support the pregnancy and your marriage?"

"Yes."

"Tell me about them."

"My father walked out on us before I was born," Madelyn said matter-of-factly. "So my mother was hesitant about me marrying Tim, but she supported my decision and was ecstatic about the twins."

"How about Tim? Did he want children?"

"We hadn't exactly planned on children so soon, but he acted happy about the pregnancy."

"What does he do for a living?"

"I'm not sure what he's doing now. When we were married, Tim was a salesman for a hardware store."

"He traveled a lot?"

"All the time." Despair threatened again. "He felt horrible for not being home the night I had the accident."

"Where was he?"

"Raleigh, on business, but he rushed to the hospital as soon as he received word."

"How did he react over losing the baby?"

Madelyn massaged her temple, remembering those first shocked, grief-stricken days.

"Madelyn?"

"He was understandably upset," she said shakily. "Riddled with guilt. I think that's what eventually caused the rift between us. He couldn't get past the guilt." Her voice dropped. "Neither could I."

"It wasn't your fault," Caleb said gruffly.

Other people had assured Madelyn of the same thing, but guilt wasn't rational. She was the mother; she was supposed to protect her child at all costs.

"Tim abandoned you and Sara when you needed him most." Caleb's tone reeked of disgust.

Madelyn had long ago tried to let go of the anger. If she'd allowed it to fester, it would have clouded every moment of her day and affected Sara. And she'd vowed to be a good mother to the little baby who'd survived.

"We were no good to each other back then," Madelyn said. "I suppose it was my fault, too. I was so obsessed with being a mother and grieving that I had no time for him."

Caleb muttered a curse. "Don't blame yourself or defend the creep. Any man who leaves his wife and child is not worthy of having a family."

His words soothed the ache building in her chest from the troubling memories.

"I'm going to phone Ben in the morning to start that trace and check your phone records. You'd better get some sleep."

Their fingers brushed as she handed him the printout, and a tingle shot through her, the warmth of knowing that he'd come to her rescue tonight creating an intimacy in the small kitchen.

An intimacy she hadn't shared with anyone in ages. One she didn't dare dwell on now.

"Thank you for staying," she said quietly. "I'll leave a pillow and blanket on the sofa."

"Thanks," Caleb said. "We'll start fresh in the morning."

His gaze locked with hers, emotions flickering in its depth. The air felt charged, electric. Sensual. Filled with the kind of tension that made her pulse pound and her breasts feel heavy.

But she stifled her feelings. If Cissy was in danger, they had to hurry.

CISSY HEARD HER MOMMY'S scream, jumped out of bed and ran down the hall. The kitchen door was open, the big man hovering over her mommy.

No...

Her mommy had told the big man to leave them alone, but he'd come back.

Now he had her by the throat. Something shiny glinted in the dim light. Cissy stared at it, terrified. It was big and sharp and jagged...

A knife!

No, no, no! She wanted to scream, but the sound died in her throat. She had to do something. Help her mommy.

Think, Cissy, think.

Help, Sara, help!

The man jerked her mother around like a rag doll and flung her against the kitchen sink. Her mother pushed against him, but he slapped her in the face so hard her mother's legs buckled.

She hated the meanie. Her mommy said he was her uncle, but he'd never been nice to her. And he was always yelling at her mommy.

She had to stop him!

Cissy ran to her room to get the bat she'd gotten for her birthday. But she stumbled and tripped in the hall. Her knees hit the cold wood, her hands clawing for something to hold on to.

A cry pierced the air behind her, and she

choked on a scream herself. The man was hurting her mama. She had to get help.

But it was dark and spooky and tears burned her eyes as she crawled to her room. She swept her hand along the floor behind the doorway searching for it, but the bat was gone.

No, no, no! Where was it?

Choking back another sob, she slid on her belly and felt beneath the bed. Her fingers closed around the bat's end, and she grabbed it and ran toward the kitchen.

But another loud scream pierced the air just as she made it to the door.

"Run, Cissy!" her mother shouted.

The shiny metal thing flickered in the light. The monster swung it up and jabbed it straight into her mommy's throat.

Her mommy screamed again. Her throat gurgled. Her head fell back.

Then all Cissy saw was red....

Chapter Eight

Sara's terrified scream cut through Madelyn like a knife, and she jerked from sleep, jumped from bed and raced across the hall. Another nightmare?

Or could the man who'd threatened her have sneaked in?

Caleb's boots pounded up the steps, and he reached out his arm to push her behind him, then scanned the dark room.

A ribbon of sunlight peeked through the blinds, and Madelyn searched the room, as well. Nothing.

Except Sara was thrashing in the sheets again, sobs racking her body.

"It's clear," he said, then stepped aside for her to enter.

Her heart in her throat, Madelyn rushed toward her daughter.

"No, no, no…" Sara cried. "Run, Cissy, run!" Sara twisted back and forth, tangling the sheets around her. Tears flowed down her little face. "Go the other way. Hurry! He's gonna get you!"

Madelyn gently shook Sara. "Honey, wake up. You're dreaming again."

Another scream pierced the air, and Sara's body convulsed with fear. "Run, Cissy!"

"Sara," Madelyn said more firmly. "Please wake up. You're safe, honey."

But Sara beat her fists at Madelyn's chest, lost in the throes of the nightmare. Madelyn hugged her daughter, swaying her back and forth. "Shh, honey, Mommy's here. I won't let anyone hurt you."

The lamp flickered on, casting a faint glow across the room, and she glanced at Caleb, tears blurring her eyes. Her little girl was in agony and Madelyn felt helpless.

Caleb inched toward her, his big body filling the room with his presence as he placed a comforting hand on her shoulder.

"Cissy, hide…" Sara whimpered. "No, mister, please, don't hurt her!"

Madelyn's throat ached. She wanted to scream that it wasn't fair for Sara to be plagued with these nightmares. Why hadn't God given her this second sight instead of little Sara? "Honey, wake up and talk to Mommy."

Slowly Sara stirred from the dream, her body trembling. A terrified, glazed look clouded her eyes.

"Sara, look, it's Mommy. And Caleb is here, too." Madelyn cradled Sara, rocking her again. "You're safe in your room and no one is going to hurt you."

Shock and fear etched itself on Sara's small face. "But Mommy… He killed Cissy's mama… He had a knife…then it was red…so red…red everywhere…" Sara's voice cracked. "And now he's got Cissy, and he's gonna kill her, too."

CALEB CLENCHED HIS JAW at the fear in the child's voice.

Madelyn's teary-eyed look sent a wave of unexpected feelings over him. More than anything, he wanted to help her and Sara.

Maybe somehow it would make up for failing his own family.

He knelt by the bed and pulled one of Sara's tiny hands in his. Suddenly the images from Sara's mind filled his own. A dark crimson stain bled across the floor. The knife glinted in the dark, the jagged blade carving a hole in the woman's throat. Then splatters of red spurted from her neck and dripped down her body.

Blood. It was everywhere.

His heart thrummed. He squeezed Sara's hand, hoping to deepen the connection. "Tell me what you see, Sara."

Sara made a strangled sound and clutched his hand tighter. Once again the images in her mind appeared in his as if a camera was showing him live feed. The red grew brighter, stronger, filling up the space in her mind. Then sounds and scents flooded him as if she was reliving the gruesome murder.

A loud scream pierced the air. A woman's. The sound of a struggle. A glass breaking. A man's grunt. Another scream from the woman, shrill with pain. The metallic scent of blood assaulted him along with the other acrid odors of death.

A little girl's gasp followed, low, scared. Shocked.

What else?

He tried to hone in on everything in the room, but he could only see through Sara's eyes. And at the moment, Sara was in shock over the sight of the blood.

"Sara, I know it's dark and it's red. Really red." He lowered his voice to a soothing pitch. "But try to drag your eyes away from the red. Look around the room, at the man and tell us what else you saw."

Madelyn's fingernails dug into his arm, disapproving, desperate. "Caleb stop. She needs to forget about it, not remember."

Caleb met Madelyn's agonized gaze. "If what she's seeing is real, the only way to make the nightmares end is to find Cissy and save her."

Surprise flickered in Madelyn's eyes as if she'd just realized that he believed Sara when no one else did. Then turmoil, because if Sara was right, her sister was in terrible danger.

That meant they had to encourage her to talk.

"Sara, baby," Madelyn said softly. "It's important. Where is Cissy? Is she with her mommy?"

Sara shook her head. "I don't know. I can't see her anymore."

"What happened when she saw the red?" Caleb asked. "Where was she?"

"In the hall by the kitchen."

"Now look up past the red, past the floor. Do you see the man?"

Sara nodded, a tremor making her body shake. "His hand?"

"His hand? What else?"

"A knife," she whispered. "It's shiny and sharp and the red… It's dripping from the end.…"

Caleb silently cursed. So the image he'd seen

in his mind was the same as Sara's visions. She'd witnessed the poor woman's murder.

Sucking in a calming breath, he rubbed Sara's hand. Her skin was clammy, her hand jittery. "Look past the knife, Sara. Do you see the man's face?"

Suddenly Sara released a wail, buried her head in her mommy's chest and the connection between her and Caleb was lost. "No," Sara cried. "I don't wants to see him. He's a monster."

"I know, Sara, but you're safe here, and I know you want to help Cissy, don't you?" Caleb said gently.

She gulped. "Yes."

Caleb wiped a tear from her cheek with his thumb. "If we know what this man looks like, we can catch him, honey."

Sara hiccupped on another sob. "He's mean and ugly and gots big hands."

Caleb gave Madelyn a sympathetic look as she soothed her little girl. He hated pushing the child, but any detail she offered might help.

"Sara," he said quietly. "Why don't you rest with your mommy for a while. Then when you feel better, maybe you can draw some pictures of the man. Okay?"

Sara nodded, and clung to her mother, obviously terrified the man might come and hurt them, as well.

If Sara was right and the killer had murdered Cissy's adopted mother, he must be getting rid of everyone who could nail him for the kidnapping.

Which meant he might come after Sara and Madelyn.

Caleb stepped into the hallway then removed his cell phone from the clip on his belt and punched in the number for GAI. They needed to find out if any women with five-year-old daughters had been reported murdered.

Every second counted.

MADELYN'S STOMACH KNOTTED with fear. Cissy might be running from a crazed killer this very second.

She wanted to scream and cry and rail against the injustice. What if they weren't doing enough? What if they didn't find Cissy in time?

Guilt mingled with terror. If only she'd trusted Sara earlier and insisted on exhuming that coffin herself. Then maybe she could have discovered the truth and found Cissy before...

Don't give up. If Sara had a connection with Cissy, Sara would know if it was too late....

Sara sniffled, her breath choppy. Poor baby.

Madelyn tucked a strand of hair behind Sara's ear. "You are such a courageous little girl, Sara," Madelyn said softly. "I know you're scared and what you saw was awful. But you're brave to tell Caleb and me about it."

Sara clung to her. "I wants to find her, Mommy. To saves her."

"Oh, baby…" Madelyn almost choked herself. "We will find her." God, she prayed she was right. How would Sara survive if they didn't?

How would she?

Feeling helpless, she sagged against the chair. Then Sara reached up and kissed her cheek. "I loves you, Mommy. I don't wants to ever lose you."

Anger suffused Madelyn. Her five-year-old should be contemplating what game to play next, planning tea parties with her friends, thinking about learning to ride her bike without training wheels, and sledding down the big hill during the next snowfall, not about death and murder and monster men attacking her.

"Don't you worry, precious." She kissed away her daughter's tears. "Mommy will always be here with you."

Sara studied her for a long moment, then took a deep breath, pushed away and straightened as if she'd gotten a bolt of courage. "I'm ready to draw that picture now."

Madelyn cradled her daughter's face in her hands. She was so beautiful that her heart ached. "Are you sure? You don't have to do anything you don't want to do."

Sara pursed her lips in a stubborn gesture that Madelyn recognized well.

"Yes, Mommy. I need my crayons and paper."

"All right. Go get them."

Sara scooted off the bed and raced over to her craft table with a determined gleam in her eyes.

"Mommy's going to make coffee while you get started," Madelyn said. "Is that all right?"

Sara nodded, and studied the paper as if trying to decide where to begin. Madelyn didn't want to leave her alone for long, but she hadn't slept well either and needed some caffeine so she hurried down the steps.

Caleb stood at the kitchen window looking out, yet he must have heard her footsteps because he turned around, his phone pressed to his ear. His gaze met hers, his eyes stormy.

Then his gaze raked down her body, over the flannel shirt to her bare legs, and she suddenly felt naked.

As if he was literally touching her with his eyes.

Shivering at the mere thought of his hands on her bare skin, Madelyn crossed her arms, wishing she'd donned a robe.

Self-recriminations quickly followed. Good heavens, what Caleb thought of her should be the last thing on her mind. Cissy's life depended on them.

Caleb's jaw snapped tight, and he glanced away, speaking low into the phone, and she quickly set the coffee to brew and retrieved a couple of hand-painted mugs from the cabinet.

"Thanks, Gage," Caleb said. "I'll discuss it with Madelyn."

He ended the call, then turned back to her, his professional look tacked into place as if they hadn't shared an intimate moment earlier. "Coffee smells good."

She tapped her fingers on the counter. "Did you sleep?"

"Some. I hope you don't mind," he said, "but I keep a duffel bag with clean clothes in my car. I grabbed a shower down here to clean up."

"That's fine." Lord help her. He looked fresh and sexy with his damp hair brushing his collar.

"Sara all right?"

"She's terrified. But she's drawing that picture now."

Caleb eyes flickered with admiration. "She's a brave little girl, Madelyn."

"I know." Madelyn's throat thickened. "But I don't want her to have to be brave. I want her to be a child, to have fun...."

Caleb moved toward her to comfort her, but Madelyn threw up a warning hand. If he touched her now, if he held her, she might completely fall apart.

Either that or beg him to never leave her.

Neither one would help them find Cissy. And finding her was all that mattered.

She gestured to his phone as he tucked it into his belt. "What are you supposed to discuss with me?"

He sighed. "I'm going to track down those couples on the list today. If you want to go, Gage suggested we drop Sara at his house to play with his little girl, Ruby. His wife Leah loves kids, and it might do Sara good to distract her for a while."

His sensitivity touched her. "That sounds like a good idea." She jerked her head toward the doorway. "I should get back. I hate for her to be alone."

He nodded, then surprised her by brushing her hair back with his hand. "I understand this is difficult, Madelyn, but she's a tough little girl."

His gaze darkened, fastening so intently on her face that Madelyn squirmed.

"She's just like her mother," he finished. "She'll be okay."

Madelyn's throat thickened at his praise. If only her husband had seen Sara that way. Instead he'd bought into her psychosis and deserted them.

Unable to reply for fear she'd reveal how much his comment meant to her, she simply nodded, then reached for the coffee mug. But she felt his gaze on her as she poured herself some coffee, added sweetener and turned to go back upstairs.

He filled the other mug, then followed her, making her body tingle with awareness. She should have gotten her robe, shouldn't have looked into his eyes and seen that spark of heat.

But as she walked into Sara's room and spotted the crimson splatters her daughter had drawn, her breath hitched. The dead woman lay on the floor in the middle of the blood, the crude drawing of the killer erasing all thoughts of heat and Caleb's eyes.

Sara's description of the man as being a monster was mirrored in the sketch. Madelyn studied the details—his face was round, and Sara had added stray marks that gave him a wooly look suggesting he had a beard. A long, jagged line ran across the upper right side of his forehead. A scar?

Her heart pounded. For a brief second, the man looked familiar.

Clenching the coffee mug with a white-knuckled grip, she tried to remember if she'd seen him before, but the brief image in her mind faded, and she couldn't put her finger on anything specific.

Then again, Sara's crude drawing might not be accurate at all. Certainly not enough for an ID.

Still, what if she had seen the man? What if he lived around Sanctuary or had been lurking around town? Maybe he'd shopped in her own store?

No… She would have remembered customers…

Her nerves pinged. Dear God. He could have been at the grocery store or the park or even the library.

And if he was watching, he'd know she hadn't called off her search.

THEY HAD EXHUMED THE COFFIN. And now they knew it was empty.

Damn Madelyn. She should have heeded his warning. But he'd watched her house all night, and he had planted a bug on her phone, and the bitch wasn't giving up. She'd called that private investigator the minute he'd hung up.

He balled his hands into fists. She would be sorry for making that call.

Hell, he didn't want to hurt the kid.

But he had to protect himself and his family.

That meant he had to tie up all loose ends.

Dammit, it was her fault the others had to die. Her fault if she lost her little girl this time.

Hunching in his coat, he slunk back to his car and headed toward the funeral home. Five years ago, Howard Zimmerman had needed money just like him. And he'd done his part and kept quiet.

But now?

If the police linked that wimpy funeral director to the kidnapping, he might spill his guts.

Laughter bubbled in his throat. The wimpy moron wouldn't get the chance.

Chapter Nine

Caleb was anxious to start tracking down the couples on the list Ben had given him, so he rustled up some eggs and toast while he waited on Madelyn and Sara. He figured they needed time alone, and he hoped Sara could offer some clue through her sketches as to Cissy's location and the identity of the killer.

He had just poured some orange juice for the three of them when they entered the kitchen. Madelyn's look of surprise made his pulse jump.

"You cooked?" she asked.

He shrugged. "Thought we could use something to eat before we get started today."

Sara plopped into a chair, then dug the spoon into the jelly jar and spread a glob on her toast while Madelyn showed him Sara's drawings. He glanced at them but refrained from asking questions until Sara had a chance to eat. Madelyn even managed a few bites herself, although anxiety riddled her every movement.

"Brush your teeth and get dressed, Sara," Madelyn said after handing Sara a napkin. "We're going to drop you off to play with a little girl named Ruby. She's the daughter of one of Caleb's friends."

Sara looked wary. "But I wants to go with you to find Cissy."

Madelyn folded her napkin into a tiny square. "Honey, Caleb and I need to do this alone today."

Caleb wiped jelly off his mouth. "You'll like Ruby, Sara. And I promise to bring your mother back safe and sound."

Reluctantly Sara agreed and lumbered up the steps to dress. Caleb studied the drawings. "Did Sara relay any more details about this man or where her sister might be?"

"Not really." Madelyn sighed, then gestured at the sketch of the man's face. "Just that he had a beard. And the line on his forehead is a scar."

"That's helpful," Caleb said. "Did Cissy ever call the man by name?"

"No. And when I asked her to draw a picture of Cissy's mommy and daddy, she said she'd never seen Cissy's daddy."

Hmm. The sketch indicated the woman had

short reddish hair. Brown eyes. And she was slightly plump. Other than that, there was nothing distinctive.

"How about her name?" Caleb asked.

"No." Frustration lined Madelyn's face. "Cissy just calls her Mommy."

Of course.

"Madelyn, when I first talked to Sara, she mentioned that she and Cissy shared secrets. Can you try to find out what those secrets are?"

Madelyn scraped the scraps into the trash, then began loading the dishwasher. "You think there might have been abuse?"

Caleb shrugged, hating the fear and horror he'd planted in Madelyn's mind. But Sara's comment about secrets had needled him. "I don't know. The girls might have been discussing which boy they liked at preschool. On the other hand, it might be a lead. Maybe there's a special place they visit, or the name of that preschool or a family member that might lead us to their location."

"Right, I hadn't thought of that. I'll talk to Sara."

Caleb's cell phone buzzed. The caller ID showed it was Amanda Peterson, so he excused himself and answered the call while Madelyn went to help Sara dress.

"Caleb, I spoke with the hospital. Dr. Emery claimed Madelyn refused an autopsy. But get this. The medical examiner didn't sign off on the death certificate—Dr. Emery did."

"What about the funeral director?"

"His name is Howard Zimmerman. He's still with the local funeral home," Amanda said. "Do you want me to pay him a visit?"

"No, I'll stop by there then track down the couples on the list Ben gave me." He paused. "Thanks, Amanda. Maybe you could check with Derek's wife and see if her contacts with the adoption agency have a lead. Also, check with the Department of Children and Family Services. Perhaps they've had reports of abuse regarding a little girl named Cissy."

"I'm on it. Oh, and by the way, Caleb, forensics didn't find anything in that coffin. No skin cells, DNA, no sign at all that a body had ever been placed inside."

Good news, Caleb thought.

But the images from Sara's nightmare taunted him. Cissy had survived five years ago.

But her time might be running out now.

MADELYN STUDIED LEAH AND Gage's home; the sense that they were a happy, trustworthy family was evident in the way the couple exchanged loving looks between themselves and their daughter, Ruby. On the ride over, Caleb had explained that Gage had adopted Ruby, but Madelyn would never have guessed that the little girl wasn't his own daughter.

"We can play dress up in my room." Ruby's eyes sparkled with excitement as she offered her hand to Sara. "Mommy gave me a trunk full of prom dresses and high heels. There's even a princess's tiara!"

Sara smiled, obviously torn between what sounded like a fun adventure and the search for her sister, but Madelyn gave her an encouraging pat, and Sara followed Ruby to her room.

"She's adorable," Leah said with a sincere smile. "Gage explained about her twin. I'm so sorry, Madelyn. We went through a terrible scare with Ruby a while back. I still wake up in a cold sweat just thinking about it."

"Thank you." Madelyn fidgeted, picking at an invisible piece of lint on her jacket. "I appreciate you watching Sara today."

"No problem." Leah rubbed her swollen abdomen. "Ruby loves playmates. And Sara needs a friend right now, too."

Madelyn sighed. "I've tried to do everything I can to protect her, but what if I fail?"

"You won't," Leah assured her. "Gage and

Caleb are on your side now. They'll find your other daughter."

But what if she was too late? If Cissy's adopted mother was dead, who was protecting Cissy now?

Madelyn forced the negative thoughts aside. She could not think like that. "When are you due?"

Leah grinned. "Six weeks. We're having a boy this time."

Gage pulled Leah up against him with a proud grin. "Little girls are special, but I have to admit I can't wait to have a son and take him fishing."

Leah poked him. "Hey, Ruby and I like to fish, too."

They laughed and Madelyn's heart clenched. They obviously loved each other dearly and were a happy family. She wanted that for Sara and Cissy.

And for the first time in her life, she wanted it for herself.

Her gaze shot to Caleb, and an image of him holding her, kissing her, looking at her and the twins with love filled her head.

Oblivious, Caleb cleared his throat. "Thanks, Leah. We really need to go. We have several leads to check out."

Madelyn wrung her hands. "I'm not sure what time we'll be back."

"Don't worry. If it's late, Sara can sleep over. Tonight's movie night anyway. We usually make popcorn and spread sleeping bags out on the floor."

Exactly what she'd like to be doing with her daughter.

Madelyn glanced anxiously at Ruby's room. "I hope Sara won't be a problem. She's been having terrible nightmares."

Leah squeezed her hands. "All the more reason for you to skedaddle and find her sister so those nightmares will end."

Madelyn nodded. That was the best thing she could do for Sara.

Gage walked them out to the car. "I talked to the sheriff," Gage said. "He agreed to inform us about any reported female murders in the state that fit our profile."

Caleb jangled his keys. "Thanks. Although he should expand that to include neighboring states. We have no idea if the couple who adopted Cissy stayed in North Carolina or moved."

"True. I'll talk to him and ask him to widen the search. Ben is also checking."

The details in Sara's sketches nagged at Madelyn. "I don't know if this means anything, but

Cissy has been drawing sunflowers. Once, she depicted her sister hiding in a building with sunflowers growing inside."

Caleb quirked his mouth in thought. "Like a hothouse."

Gage's interest perked up. "I'll ask Slade to check on that angle. A specific type of greenhouse might help narrow down the location where the mother lives or works."

Madelyn climbed in the car, knotting her hands in her lap as Caleb drove them to the funeral home. The brick building with its adjoining chapel stirred painful memories of the memorial service she'd held for Cissy. She'd been in shock, grief stricken, and recovering from the C-section.

Yet now she knew her daughter hadn't been dead.

"I can't believe Dr. Emery lied to me and that he persuaded other people to cover for him."

Caleb's strong jaw twitched as he parked. "If Zimmerman was involved, he'll pay."

But justice would not replace the years she'd lost with her child.

She pushed aside the thought and squared her shoulders. She had to be strong. Focus on the future.

Together she and Caleb walked up to the front

door of the funeral parlor. The bare flowerbeds mocked her. Ironically it had been the first day of spring when she'd held Cissy's memorial service. The azaleas had glowed with color, the air fragrant with spring. She'd stood in this very spot and wondered how she could possibly bury a child on such a beautiful day.

But she hadn't buried her. She'd buried an empty casket.

Renewed anger fortified her, and she shoved her way through the door. Inside, the scent of cleaning chemicals mingled with the sickening-sweet aroma of roses. The same soft elevator music echoed through the intercom, grating on her nerves.

A quick inventory of the interior, and she noted that the decor hadn't changed, either. Seating areas in grays and burgundy offered conversation areas to mourners, an office to the right served as the headquarters for the director and four viewing rooms flanked the hallway. Though usually at least one of them held a casket and was overflowing with visitors, this morning all four were empty, giving the place an eerie, morbid feel.

Caleb veered toward the office where a young, blond man in his early twenties sat doing paperwork. Caleb knocked. "Excuse me, we need to speak to Howard Zimmerman."

The young man stood, fastening his dark suit jacket. "I'm his son, Roy. Maybe I can help you? Are you here for a consultation about a lost loved one?"

Caleb's gaze cut across the sterile surroundings. "No, we really must speak with Howard. Is he here?"

Roy shifted, obviously curious now. "He's downstairs. I can get him for you if you'll just tell me what this is about."

Madelyn tried lamely to wrestle her emotions under control. But the cloying scents of the roses and memories of grief-filled faces and voices haunted her.

"It's regarding a missing child case." Caleb flashed his GAI identification. "Now lead the way, and we'll follow."

Roy looked uncertain, but Caleb's voice had been commanding, and his size obviously intimidated the young man, so he motioned for them to follow him down a flight of stairs, then a dark hall. The scent of formaldehyde, alcohol, bleach and other chemicals reeked from the end room, obviously meant to mask the stench of death, but failing.

Roy cracked the door and glanced inside, then

shook his head. "Not in there. He must be inventorying the coffins."

Nerves gathered along Madelyn's spine, a chilling bleakness filling the air. Then Roy veered to the left and opened a set of double doors. Inside, caskets in various shades of gray, bronze and silver lined the room. Roy flicked on the overhead light making Madelyn blink against the sudden brightness.

Then Roy gasped and staggered backward.

Madelyn peered around him, and bile rose to her throat.

Howard Zimmerman was sprawled inside a pewter casket, his limbs askew, his chest torn open by a bullet wound, blood soaking the white satin bedding and pillow.

CALEB SHOVED MADELYN BEHIND him and out the door.

"Dad?" Roy's face turned a pasty white, and he stumbled forward toward the body, but Caleb blocked him.

"No, Roy, don't touch anything. This is a crime scene."

"My father..." Roy doubled over with shock and grief, then started to shake.

Madelyn pulled herself together faster than he would have imagined and gently gripped Roy's arm. "Come on, Roy. Step into the hall and take a deep breath."

Not that the hallway was any less of a reminder of death. The scents of chemicals permeated the floors and walls. The overwhelming feeling of grief and death and lost spirits lingered, their whispers taunting him. Angry spirits. Lost souls. Ones hanging in limbo and desperate for redemption. Others determined to exact revenge for a life cut short.

Then others who simply weren't ready to accept their fate and let go of loved ones.

Was that the reason Mara's spirit hovered by her grave? Was she angry with him? Or was she ready to move on but needed some kind of closure with him?

For a moment, he wondered if that could be the case between Sara and Cissy, if Cissy had already passed. Was her spirit hanging on, needing Sara to find her murderer so she could rest in peace?

No. He had to remain positive.

Sara's images had been reflected in his own mind. He'd heard Cissy's screams and felt her terror as if she was very much alive.

A low, keening sound erupted from Roy, jerking Caleb from his thoughts.

Madelyn helped the undertaker into a chair, and Roy leaned over, his elbows on his knees, gasping for air as if he might faint.

Caleb glanced back at Howard and silently cursed. Dammit, another lead gone.

How had the killer known they were going to question Nadine and Howard? Was there anyone else on his hit list?

Caleb punched the sheriff's number. "Sheriff Gray, this is Caleb Walker. I'm at the funeral home. Howard Zimmerman is dead."

"I'll be right there." Sheriff Gray's breath quickened as if he was hurrying outside. "What happened?"

Caleb explained his suspicions about the exhumation and funeral home. "Howard's son Roy brought us downstairs to speak to his father, but we found his body in one of the caskets."

"Damn," Sheriff Gray muttered. "Seems like everyone connected to Emery and the adoptions is being killed off."

"Yeah, someone is determined not to leave any witnesses behind." Caleb remembered the threat to Madelyn and Sara.

But the bastard would not hurt either one of them. Not unless he killed Caleb first.

HE CURSED AS HE WATCHED little Sara Andrews playing with Gage McDermont's kid. The damn P.I. was watching them like a freaking hawk.

He'd never get the kid without getting caught.

Hell. He dropped his head into his hands and groaned. What was he going to do?

Nadine was dead and now Zimmerman was, too.

Two off his list.

And Cissy's mother. Number three. Stupid bitch shouldn't have started asking questions. He'd warned her, but just like Madelyn, she hadn't listened.

What to do with Cissy though... That was the big question.

He studied the P.I. and the kids again, then considered his options. Madelyn loved family more than anything. The fool woman would throw herself in front of a bus to protect her babies.

She had another family member that she worshipped, too.

Her mother.

He'd already researched her. Knew her phone number. Her address. Where she shopped. Who administered her meds at that senior home.

And when the woman was alone.

A grin curled his lips. He knew exactly how to force Madelyn to do as he ordered.

She'd learn the hard way.

He didn't like it, but it had to be.

Bye-bye Mama…

Chapter Ten

Although Roy Zimmerman was visibly distraught over his father's murder, Caleb approached him as a suspect. Being upset or even in shock didn't negate the fact that he might have information.

"Roy." Caleb crossed his arms and faced the young man. "We need to talk about your father."

Roy squinted through the bright morning sunlight. Around them trees swayed in the wind and a flock of birds flew above, heading farther south.

"He's dead," Roy said in a high-pitched voice. "Why would someone kill Daddy?"

"That's what I'd like to know," Caleb said. "Maybe we should go into your office."

Roy's brows furrowed in confusion, and he led them back to his office like a kid who needed to be told what to do.

"Are you sure we should question him now?" Madelyn asked in a low voice. "He's in shock."

"If he's hiding something, it's better to catch him before he has time to think about it." And plan a cover-up.

Madelyn's eyes flickered with understanding, and they stepped inside Zimmerman's office. Roy filled a paper cup with water from the dispenser in the corner and slumped down in the desk chair, his hand shaking as he drank.

Madelyn claimed one of the chairs and Caleb settled his bulk in the other one, facing Roy. "Roy, we're investigating a possible kidnapping from five years ago with Mrs. Andrews." Caleb gestured toward Madelyn. "We suspect your father had information that could help us."

Clearly confused, Roy glanced back and forth between them. "Do we have to do this now?"

Caleb sensed the man's rising panic. "The sheriff is on his way, Roy. But this case might be related to your father's murder."

Roy crunched the paper cup and tossed it into the trash. "What are you talking about?"

Caleb forced himself to tread slowly. He didn't want to spook Roy; he wanted to reel him in. "Did you work here with your father five years ago?"

Roy shook his head. "No. I was away at

school." Suspicion filled his eyes. "Why? What is this about?"

"Does your dad have financial problems?" Caleb asked instead of answering.

"No." Roy indicated the funeral parlor with a sweep of one narrow hand. "The business has done well."

"How about five years ago? Any problems back then?"

Roy's complexion paled slightly. "No," he stammered, although this time his response had a false ring to it. "Why do you want to know?"

Caleb explained about the twins' birth and the exhumation. "So you see, Roy, someone here, your father probably, buried that empty casket, and we want to know who put him up to it."

Roy shot up from his seat, his eyes twitching. "My father would never do something like that. He was an upstanding citizen. In the Rotary Club. A friend of the mayor."

"We believe he did," Caleb said, standing as well, and bracing himself in case the man turned violent. "It's possible someone paid him to cover up the fact that there was no body."

"No…" Roy shook his head vehemently. "How dare you bad-mouth my father. For God's sake, his body isn't even cold and you're accusing him of a crime!"

"Think about it, Roy," Caleb said sharply. "Your father's murder wasn't random. Someone had a reason, a motive, to murder him. Do you know what it was?"

"I have no idea," Roy's voice cracked with disbelief. "My father is a good man. He wouldn't do anything illegal."

Caleb sighed. "Roy, maybe you are innocent. But we believe your father was murdered to keep him from talking to us."

Roy shook his head in denial. "No, you're wrong."

"Please," Madelyn cut in. "Somebody stole my baby, Roy. And I think she's in danger now. Help us find her."

Roy swallowed hard as his gaze veered toward Madelyn. "I'm sorry but I can't." He swung his hand toward Caleb. "Now, this conversation is over."

"It's not over." Caleb jammed his face into Roy's. "And it won't be until we find Madelyn's missing child. So if you know anything about it, then step up. Because if you're covering for your father, I'll make sure you're charged with accessory, and your butt will go to jail."

SIRENS SCREECHED OUTSIDE. Roy shouted at Caleb and Madelyn to leave again, so they went outside to meet the sheriff.

Needing some fresh air, Madelyn waited on the park bench as Caleb relayed their conversation with Roy and how they'd discovered Howard's corpse. Then he accompanied the sheriff inside to the crime scene.

She shivered as the cool breeze rustled trees and tossed drying leaves to the ground.

Poor Roy. He was devastated.

And Howard… She had mixed feelings about his death. On a basic human level, it disgusted her that he'd been shot in cold blood. But his murder suggested he had been involved in Cissy's disappearance.

Damn him.

She balled her hands into fists. How could all these people have lied to her? How could they have stolen her child and allowed her to believe her baby was dead? That was beyond cruel.…

Caleb strode outside, the sight of him automatically filling her with relief. He looked so big and strong and formidable, that she wanted to melt in his arms and let him make the horrid memory of all that blood fade.

He gave her a concerned look, then slid down beside her and spread his hands on his knees.

"They're searching for forensics, but the medical examiner puts Zimmerman's death at around 11:00 p.m."

A shudder coursed through Madelyn. "Then he's been lying there all night?"

"Yes." Caleb wrapped an arm around her. Immediately his warmth seeped through her, warding off the chill from the wind and the memory of seeing Howard's bulging eyes staring up at them in death.

"I can't believe this is happening. Two people murdered," Madelyn whispered.

Caleb cupped her face in his hands. "It must mean that we're on to something, Madelyn. Try to hold on to that fact."

She nodded, then looked into his dark eyes. Compassion, worry and determination flickered in the depths, along with a sensitivity that made her pulse pound.

A sliver of desire sparked, heating her blood and making her yearn to lean into him even more. To place her lips on his and taste his sexy mouth.

But noises intruded, reminding her that a dead man lay inside, quickly obliterating any fantasies of kissing Caleb and having him return that kiss.

"The sheriff sent his deputy to Zimmerman's

house with another forensics team. Maybe they'll find a lead for us." Caleb glanced into the woods surrounding the funeral home. "I also called Ben, and he's checking Zimmerman's financials."

"Even if you find something, what good will it do now?" Madelyn asked. "He's dead. He can't tell us where Cissy is."

Caleb rubbed her arms. "A paper trail could lead us to the killer or whoever hired him," Caleb said. "And we want concrete evidence to be able to nail him in court."

"Right." Madelyn wasn't thinking about court. Only finding Cissy. "I should check on Sara."

"Done. Gage is staying with the girls and Leah to make sure Sara is safe."

Madelyn sighed in relief. It had been so long since anyone had taken care of her and Sara that it felt oddly unsettling. Uncomfortable in one regard and blissful in another. But she couldn't allow herself to grow accustomed to it. Still, for now, it was nice. "Thank you, Caleb."

His gaze softened. "I told you I'd protect you and find the truth and I keep my promises."

"I guess I'm not accustomed to men I can count on," she said, then wished she hadn't revealed so much.

He rubbed the back of her neck with his

thumb, and a frisson of something sweet and sensual rippled between them. "Not every man is your ex, Madelyn. Some of us care about family and honor, about protecting women and children."

Madelyn desperately wanted to believe him. All the agents at GAI must care about families or they wouldn't have dedicated their careers to finding missing children. "But you don't have a family of your own?"

Intense pain flashed in his eyes so quickly that it sucked the air from Madelyn's lungs. Then a shuttered look fell across his face, and he pulled away as if she'd crossed some invisible line.

"Since the police have the crime scene covered, we should get moving," he said, back to business.

"I'm sorry if I said something wrong, Caleb." Madelyn touched his arm, needing to apologize, to make up for whatever she'd said to upset him, but he launched himself to his feet and slanted her a look that warned her that the conversation was over.

"The first couple on Ben's list lives about an hour from here." He headed to his Jeep and she raced to catch up with him.

"Their names are Bill and Ava Butterworth." His keys jangled in his hands. "He's an accountant. She's a pharmacist but gave up her job to stay home with the kids."

Madelyn missed the intimacy she'd felt between them. But he was right to keep their relationship focused on the case.

Still, the anguish in his eyes haunted her. Caleb had his own secrets. Secrets he obviously didn't want to share. Secrets that had hurt him deeply.

And for once, instead of thinking about her own pain, she wanted to alleviate his.

CALEB REALIZED HE'D BEEN rude by cutting Madelyn off, but he wasn't prepared to discuss the loss of his wife and child, not with her.

Not with anyone.

Guilt plagued him for the momentary spark of attraction he'd felt for her. He could not allow himself to fantasize about holding her or having her. And he sure as hell didn't deserve for her to look at him as if he was a savior when he hadn't been able to save his own family.

But he'd do his best to save hers.

She lapsed into silence as he drove from town onto the highway leading to Hopewell, the small town where Ava and Bill Butterworth lived. Mountains fanned out, the rolling hills and valleys picturesque, although those same ridges and cliffs offered hiding places for those who didn't want to be found.

It was nearly noon by the time they crawled into the town. Signs for winter sales filled shops while people hunched in their coats and hurried from their cars to their destinations, too rushed and cold to stop and chat.

He followed the GPS directions down a small side street that led to an older subdivision, the houses a mixture of wood cottages and brick ranches. Children's bicycles, outdoor play equipment and remnants of a snowman painted it as a family neighborhood.

Caleb parked in front of a gray, well-kept, one-story house with white shutters and sprawling oaks that swept the ground with yards of Spanish moss.

Madelyn twisted her hands. "God, Caleb. What if this couple has Cissy? What do we do?"

His hands tightened around the steering wheel. If Sara was right, they might walk in and find another dead body.

"We'll cross that bridge when we come to it," he replied.

Madelyn gritted her teeth, then opened her car door. He slid from the driver's side, circled the front of the car to her and placed his hand at the small of her back for reassurance as they made their way up the pebbled path to the front door. Caleb's mind ticked over the details of the history Ben had printed out on the couple. From the looks of the Butterworth's financials, their house and the van parked in the drive, the couple appeared to be a normal, middle-class family.

One who wouldn't welcome his questions, even if they hadn't adopted Cissy. Of course, no adopted parent wanted their histories dug up or exposed.

He didn't blame them, especially if they were legitimate and innocent and had been deceived themselves.

But he approached with caution. Who knew what secrets lay behind closed doors?

Madelyn ran her fingers through her hair. "Do we tell them who we are?"

Caleb contemplated that question. Being honest might work in their favor or send people running. Either way, Sara and Cissy were identical twins, so Madelyn would recognize her child if she was here.

"Let's just feel them out," he said. He rang the doorbell and they waited several seconds. The sound of voices echoed from behind the door, then the door opened and a brunette stood in the doorway with a baby on her hip. Behind her, two more children appeared, somewhere between the ages of two and four, then a tow-headed child about five joined them, jelly streaking her mouth.

"Can I help you?" The woman ushered the kids behind her in a protective gesture.

But they tugged and shouted at her. "Mommy, we want cookies."

"When are we going to Nana's?"

"Jamie looked at me."

"I did not."

"He did, too."

Ava rolled her eyes. "Enough, Jacob and Jamie. Hang on a minute."

Caleb cleared his throat and glanced at Madelyn who was intently studying the oldest child.

"My name is Caleb Walker." He presented his identification. "I'm with a private investigative firm called GAI."

She spun around and directed her comment to the oldest child. "Esme, take the others into the kitchen. Hand out the sandwiches. I'll be there in a minute."

Esme gave her mother an obedient smile, then gathered the bickering brood and shooed them toward the kitchen. "Come on, cookies for dessert!"

After they skedaddled away, Ava turned back to them. "I don't know how I can help you."

"I hired him," Madelyn softly cut him off. "Five years ago, I gave birth to twins at Sanctuary Hospital, but Dr. Emery told me one of them died. Recently I learned that wasn't true. I believe he sold my baby to a couple who adopted her, and I'm trying to locate them now."

Panic stretched across Ava's face. "I heard about Dr. Emery's death and the accusations against him, but Esme is not your child." Her throat worked as she swallowed. "We met the young woman who gave birth to her. Her name was Penelope, and we paid her expenses during childbirth. She was only fifteen and was grateful to find us."

"How about your other children?" Caleb asked. "Did you adopt them through Dr. Emery?"

"No." The woman gave a humorless laugh. "A month after we adopted, I learned I was pregnant. Since then, I've been a hotbed of fertility."

Madelyn chewed her bottom lip. "Did you know any of the other couples who adopted?"

"No." Ava clenched the door edge. The sound of the kids escalated. "You really believe this doctor stole your baby?"

Madelyn removed a photo of Sara from her purse. "Yes. This is my little girl Sara. She has a twin named Cissy, the baby Dr. Emery told me had died. But I buried an empty casket."

Ava's shocked gasp rattled in the silence.

"Please, if there's any way you can help us, I'd appreciate it. I think Cissy and her adopted mother are in danger." Madelyn drew a labored breath. "I want to save them both if I can."

A seed of doubt flickered in Ava's eyes. "I'm sorry," she said, her tone sincere. "But I don't know anything about your baby or where she is now."

Then she closed the door in their faces.

"What do you think?" Caleb asked.

"Esme is not Cissy," Madelyn said wearily.

"No, but we scared Ava," Caleb said. "I say we head to the others on the list before Ava has a chance to contact anyone."

Madelyn had a stricken look. "You think she knows where Cissy is?"

"Not necessarily," Caleb said. "But I don't want to take the chance just in case she's hiding something."

MADELYN CONTEMPLATED Caleb's comment as they drove the forty-five minutes to the next house on the list. This place was much more ritzy, a private estate in the mountains that belonged to a couple named Stacy and James Ingles. Judging from their property and the Mercedes and BMW parked in the three-car garage, they definitely had the money to pay for a child.

And more.

When Stacy Ingles opened the door and greeted them, Caleb quickly explained who they were and Madelyn filled in the rest.

"I'm sorry to hear your story," Stacy said. "But you have a lot of nerve invading our privacy."

"I'm not here to make trouble for you," Madelyn said.

"Mrs. Ingles," Caleb cut in. "Whoever adopted Cissy needs to know that she was kidnapped, not given up willingly."

"So you're going to tear her family's lives apart," Stacy said. "And that child's. If she's with a loving family, think what that will do to her."

Madelyn's lungs tightened. "If that's the case, we'll work together for whatever is best for Cissy," Madelyn said through gritted teeth.

Her child belonged with her. She had not given her up and she wanted her back. Sara deserved to have her sister.

"However," Caleb said sharply. "We don't

think that's the case. We have reason to believe that Cissy and her adopted mother are in danger." He explained about Nadine Cotter's and Howard Zimmerman's murders. "We're trying to save their lives."

Stacy's fingers tightened to a white-knuckled grip around the door edge as she stared at them, obviously struggling for a response. Finally she drew a deep breath. "I don't have your child, Mrs. Andrews." She walked to the table in the foyer, picked up a family photo and brought it back. The moment Madelyn saw it she knew the Ingles hadn't adopted Cissy.

Their child was Asian. "We didn't adopt through Dr. Emery," Stacy said quietly. "He referred us to an international adoption agency when our fertility treatments failed. Sue Li is from China."

Desperation tore at Madelyn's insides. "I'm sorry we bothered you."

Caleb removed a business card and pushed it into Stacy's hand. "If you think of anything that can help, a name, maybe, someone who might have a lead for us, please call me."

Stacy chewed her bottom lip but accepted the business card with a nod.

Frustration filled Madelyn as they headed back to Caleb's Jeep.

"We're not giving up, Madelyn," Caleb said.

But a thick silence fell between them as they drove away. Madelyn stared out the window at the desolate mountains, the sharp cliffs and ridges, the winter wind biting through her bones.

What if Cissy was out there now, running from that madman, lost?

The late afternoon sun was waning as they stopped at a small, barbecue restaurant, and Caleb ordered a late lunch for them both. He wolfed down two barbecue sandwiches, but she could barely force herself to eat a bite. Instead the images from Sara's drawings, the images of Nadine and Howard both lying in their own blood, taunted her.

What if Sara was right, and Cissy's adopted mother was dead, too? Would they find Cissy in time?

Nausea flooded her, and she had to force herself not to think as they walked to the car, and Caleb drove into the mountains near Boone.

"Third couple—the Peddersons," Caleb said. "Rayland Pedderson bought a mountain lodge six years ago. Wife helps him run it."

Madelyn glanced around the log cabin resort. It had obviously been designed for hunters, people who wanted to escape to a rustic, more primitive life.

Remembering Sara's sketch of the greenhouse, she glanced to the side in search of another building, but the outbuildings were individual dining halls and clubhouses for guests and special functions.

Caleb climbed out, and Madelyn followed, her legs weak as she mounted the stairs. Rocking chairs lined the front porch with checkerboards arranged strategically throughout, and the sound of the river rushing over rocks echoed from behind the lodge, slivers of sunlight slanting through the pines.

Caleb escorted her inside, the mountain theme continuing with deer, elk heads and fish mounted on the rustic walls. A gun cabinet behind the registration desk was filled with rifles and shotguns and a second cabinet in the corner held various knives.

A grunt indicated someone was behind the counter. Caleb rang the bell, and a mountain of a man suddenly stood.

"Rayland Pedderson?" Caleb called out as they approached.

"That's me." The big, burly man leaned across the registration desk, clawing beefy fingers through his thick beard.

Madelyn's heart pounded. The image Sara had drawn of the monster flashed in her head. Rayland Pedderson could be their man.

Chapter Eleven

"Would you two like a room?" Pedderson's gaze skated over Madelyn insinuating he thought their visit was a clandestine love affair.

Caleb flashed his ID. "No, thanks. We're here for information."

All friendliness fled from the man's beefy face. "Oh, hell. You're that damn P.I. and the chick asking questions about Dr. Emery."

"You were expecting us?" Caleb asked, senses alert. "Who told we were coming?"

"Don't matter," Pedderson muttered. "I can't help you."

"Can't or won't?" Caleb asked.

"Can't." Pedderson retrieved a photo from the mantle and showed them a framed five-by-seven of him, a dyed-blonde woman and a chubby, brown-haired girl with dimples. "This is me and Beatrice and little Bea."

"You adopted little Bea," Caleb said. "Through Dr. Emery?"

Pedderson yanked a rifle from below the desk. "Don't you go spreadin' rumors like that. Little Bea is *ours*." He braced the rifle on his shoulder and aimed at Caleb. "Ours, you hear me? And no one is sayin' any different and takin' her away." He gestured toward the door with the moose's head mounted above it. "Now git."

Beside Caleb, Madelyn's breath hitched. "Mr. Pedderson, please help us…"

"*Please* git," Pedderson said with a snarl that showcased tobacco-stained teeth. "And don't come back or meddle in our lives or you'll be sorry."

Caleb held up his hands to indicate they were not a threat, then led Madelyn toward the exit. Outside, she sighed against him.

"He's a nasty man and he does have a beard, but he didn't adopt Cissy."

"No," Caleb agreed. "But he may be hiding something. I'll ask Ben to keep these names on file. GAI is receiving other calls from people who claim to have been duped by Emery. If Pedderson is on the list and illegally adopted Bea, someone needs to know."

Madelyn shivered as they rushed to Caleb's SUV and headed back toward town. "It's getting late. I should pick up Sara."

"We have one more stop," Caleb said. "Don't

worry. Leah and Gage are taking care of Sara. I know it's difficult, Madelyn. But trust us to help you."

He didn't know why it was important to him that she did, but he wanted her trust. And he wanted to deliver for her more than anything he'd wanted in a long time.

"All right," she said softly. "At least now I feel like I'm finally doing something, taking action. Hopefully Sara will understand."

"She will, she's a tough little girl." Caleb squeezed her hand. "Cissy must be strong, too, Madelyn. She's reaching out to Sara. We'll find her because of that connection."

Hope filled Madelyn's haunted eyes. Damn her sorry ex-husband. Obviously she wasn't accustomed to accepting help or to people believing Sara, and he was going to do both.

Madelyn licked her lips. "Tell me about this last couple on the list."

He mentally ticked away the few details on the printout. They were, by far, the couple with the least background information, which raised suspicions in itself. "The Smiths. Husband was in the service. Wife was an admin assistant at a lawyer's office."

"Could that lawyer have handled the adoption?"

Caleb shrugged. "It's possible. But there's not much here to go on. The file is slim, which makes me wonder if Smith is an alias." Caleb followed that logic. "Hell, now that I think about it, your accident could have been a set-up. Maybe the driver sideswiped you hoping you'd go into labor, then followed you to the hospital and set the adoption in place with Emery."

Madelyn grew silent as if she'd collapsed within herself, making him desperately want to erase her pain. But they'd both known digging for answers might lead to painful truths. And there was no turning back now.

"If someone orchestrated that attack and took Cissy, he deserves to rot in jail," Madelyn said, her voice strained.

"He will pay," Caleb assured her. Although, hell, he'd like to kill the bastard himself.

Finally Madelyn closed her eyes and dozed while he wound around the mountain and crossed into Tennessee. But even in her sleep, Madelyn didn't relax. She twitched and moaned and a tear trickled down her cheek.

Caleb gently wiped it away with the pad of his thumb, then covered her hand with his. "It's going to be okay, Madelyn. You're not alone now."

Slowly she opened her eyes and looked at him. Her lost look twisted him inside out. Made him want to step up and be the man she needed.

To hold her, forget his own problems and assuage her pain.

The thought terrified him. Yet at the same time, he ached to do it, anyway. To jump in without caution.

"Are we almost there?" she asked in a low voice.

Thank God she was oblivious to his thoughts. Dangerous ones for a man who'd failed one family and didn't deserve to dream about another one.

"Yeah." He swung the SUV up the graveled road, and they bounced over the ruts, spitting dust and rocks as they barreled up the drive to the remote cabin at the top of the ridge. The wind hurled leaves and broken branches from a recent storm across the patchwork drive as he pulled to a stop. Storm clouds gathered above, rumbling and threatening sleet, and the sun disappeared, night descending.

He scanned the property, the clapboard house, the woods beyond. A stray dog barked from the woods somewhere, but there were no cars in sight.

Madelyn leaned forward, surveying the property. "This is where the Smiths live?"

"It's the latest address Ben found." But Caleb sensed Madelyn's train of thought. Any family who'd bought a child would have money. They wouldn't live in a broken-down shack like this.

Unless they were on the run. Maybe they hadn't adopted Cissy at all. Maybe they had stolen her from the hospital, and Emery had covered it up.

And if Pedderson had been warned, someone might have tipped off this couple and they'd disappeared.

Checking his gun to make sure it was still tucked into his pants, he climbed out. But his sixth sense hinted that something was wrong. So far, the body count had been piling up. He hoped to hell he wasn't about to stumble on another corpse.

Especially a woman's. Or worse, a child's. Madelyn's child.

"Caleb?" Madelyn reached for the door handle.

"Wait here, Madelyn."

She dropped her hand to her lap and looked warily around. He locked the car doors and inched forward, senses honed as he scanned left and right.

His pulse pounded as he made his way up to the cabin. The steps to the front stoop squeaked, brittle wood sagging beneath the weight of his boots, and he paused on each step, scanning all directions, braced for an attack.

But when he reached the front, a sense of desolation overwhelmed him. An emptiness. The scent of dust and mold and decay.

Wielding his gun, he peered inside the window to the right and saw no movement inside. Jaw clenched, he pushed open the door and inched inside just to make sure. Cissy had supposedly seen the mother killed in the kitchen.

The wood floor creaked as he crossed the foyer. The living area was small, a faded green sofa and plaid chair left behind, but no other furniture or signs of life. To the right he spotted a small hallway which led to the bedrooms but the kitchen adjoined the living area, separated by swinging doors. He elbowed through them and scanned the room. Worn, yellowed linoleum. Beat up cabinets. The scent of cigarette smoke and stale beer.

Empty otherwise.

Removing a penlight from his pocket, he shined it across the floor in search of blood, but detected none. Just mud stains, dust and spilled beer. Obviously Mrs. Smith wasn't a housekeeper. And there was no sign or hint of bleach used to remove blood.

Instincts sharpened, he strode to the bedrooms, expecting the worst.

But he found no body there, either.

Determined to know if they'd been here, he searched for clues as to the couple's whereabouts—mail, a note left behind, an address of a friend—but barring the metal beds in the rooms, the space had been cleaned out completely.

The Smiths had left without a trace.

THE ISOLATED LOCATION of this place made Madelyn's skin crawl. Were the couple simply outdoors people, hermits, or were they hiding from someone?

She scanned the deep, dark pockets of the forests. If Cissy lived here and had run from this madman, she could be anywhere, lost in those woods. Alone. Scared.

Maybe hurt.

Wild animals, bears, coyotes, snakes, the elements… Any one of them could be lethal to a small child. And if she hadn't escaped…

No, she couldn't allow herself to think the

worst. Couldn't let herself believe that her precious little girl was in the hands of a killer.

But she might be. Sara had seen the man murder Cissy's adopted mother.

Caleb stalked down the front steps of the porch, and she released a pained breath. His chiseled jaw was set firmly as if he had bad news, making her stomach pitch.

He flung open the car door and settled inside, reaching for his cell phone.

"What did you find?" she asked, anxiety knotting her shoulders.

He sighed warily. "Good and bad news. No one was there. No body. But no Cissy, either."

She clung to hope. "Did you see anything? Photos maybe?"

"No. There was no sign of them, nothing personal. No clothes, dishes, toys, food." He clasped her hand. "No blood, either. So if this couple is the one who adopted Cissy, they moved on."

"And if the mother was killed?"

"It didn't happen in this house," Caleb said. "There was no evidence of blood or indication that someone had cleaned up after a crime. In fact, the house was dusty, as though no one has lived here for a while."

Her optimism deflated. She hadn't wanted to find a dead woman, but she needed to know they were making progress, that they were on the right track.

"Let me phone GAI and check in." Caleb started the engine and headed down the mountain. "Maybe Ben will have some information."

She looked out the window again, the forest growing more ominous as night swallowed the horizon. She tried to wrangle her thoughts out of despair while she listened to Caleb confer with his colleague.

"Looks like this couple left a while back. Smith could be an alias, so see what else you can dig up." He paused. "Any word on Nadine's or Mansfield's phones, or a murder victim fitting our profile?" He made a low sound in his throat. "Okay, we're headed back to Sanctuary. Keep us posted."

"Any news?" Madelyn asked as soon as he ended the call.

"Nadine's phone records indicate she called this address last month shortly after Emery was arrested. Mansfield also made phone calls around the same time."

Madelyn twined her fingers in her lap. "Meaning Nadine and Mansfield both covered for Emery?"

"It looks that way."

Madelyn glanced back at the deserted house.

"Where is this couple now?" And did they have Cissy?

Caleb covered her hand with his again. "We're working on it, Madelyn. Hang in there, okay?"

Her throat closed. "I will. I just hope Cissy can."

Madelyn felt herself shutting down, physically and mentally. Caleb lapsed into silence, as well, and seemed to focus on driving. She studied his face wondering about his Native American roots.

Anything to take her mind off the fact that they might not find Cissy in time.

CALEB STEWED OVER THE last few hours, trying to piece together the truth.

"What tribe are you from?" Madelyn asked, interrupting his thoughts. "Cherokee? Apache?"

Caleb whipped his head toward her, surprised at the question. He'd thought prejudices would die with time but still occasionally encountered them. "Does it matter?"

"No, not at all," Madelyn said. "I was just curious. Trying to distract myself from worrying."

At the quiver in her voice, Caleb relaxed his steely grip on the steering wheel. So she was just making conversation. Madelyn didn't have a mean bone in her body.

But she had no idea she'd hit one of his hot buttons. "My mother was white, my father Cherokee," he said, battling bitterness. "But my mother's parents never accepted my father."

"What happened?"

Did he really want to revisit his past? "It's not important," Caleb said.

"You know everything about me, Caleb," Madelyn said softly. "I'd really like to know more about you. I think of you as a friend."

A bead of perspiration trickled down his temple. He itched to touch her but tightened his fingers around the steering wheel instead. A friend? Unfortunately he was starting to want more than that.

Starting to want Madelyn in his arms, in his life.

But friendship was all they could have.

Besides, better the subject of his cultural heritage than Mara. "My mother's parents accused my father of taking advantage of my mother. Eventually they pressured her into giving me up. My red skin embarrassed them."

"That's awful," Madelyn said. "How could your mother have given in to that pressure, though? How could she give up her child?"

Caleb glanced at her, moved that she was incensed over his mother's abandonment. "Her family was prestigious, she was young." Excuses, excuses, excuses. "I don't think she really wanted to be saddled with a child anyway."

"I can't imagine ever feeling like that," Madelyn said. "Children are a blessing and should be treasured."

He chuckled at her vehement tone. She was a barracuda when it came to kids. A trait that stirred his admiration.

He wished his own mother had been as nurturing and protective as Madelyn.

But not all women were as unselfish.

"Where's your father?" Madelyn asked.

"He died about ten years ago. A couple of bikers jumped him in an alley and beat him to death. That's when I decided to be a cop." And the reason he'd decided to marry a Native American. He didn't want his own family to endure the prejudice he'd encountered. Prejudices that had no place in modern times, but nonetheless seeped through like poison.

"He must have been very special for you to honor him that way," Madelyn said.

He simply gave a clipped nod. Let her think what she wanted. Truth was, his old man had been bitter after the way Caleb's mother had treated him, and he'd carried a chip on his shoulder that had attracted trouble.

But he'd said enough. Talking about his family and past wasn't something he intended to dwell on.

His cell phone buzzed, thankfully ending Madelyn's questions. He grabbed the phone from his belt and punched Connect. "Walker here."

"Caleb, it's Gage. I just talked to Ben. Mansfield has disappeared."

"What?"

"Don't worry, I'm with Leah and the girls and they're safe. But Ben said he heard him talking about needing a new passport."

"Under a different name?"

"That's right. Ben tried to trace the call but it was a throwaway cell. I sent Colt Mason over but Mansfield was gone. Looks like he packed up and skipped town."

"Does the sheriff know?"

"Yes. He's already issued an APB on Mansfield, but I wanted to give you a heads-up."

Caleb sighed. Dammit. Mansfield knew they were closing in on him, linking him to Cissy's kidnapping and the sketchy adoptions. And he was probably afraid whoever killed Nadine would come after him, too.

Unless he was more involved than they'd thought. Maybe he was the mastermind behind the adoption ring and he had ordered the hit on Nadine.

Either way, they had to track him down and make him talk.

THE LIGHTS WERE TURNED off at Sanctuary Seniors at ten. Just like little kids, the old folks had a bedtime. The nurses checked in. Made sure the residents took their blood pressure medicines and countless other pills. Helped them to the bathroom if they needed it. Changed their diapers if that was the case. Then tucked them in for the night.

Madelyn's mother, Cora Barker—the old bag—was probably sleeping. Snoring away like some pampered princess in her little garden suite.

Well, her peaceful sleep was about to come to an end.

Pulling the janitor's hat low on his forehead, he leaned the broom against the concrete wall, careful to keep his face averted from the security cameras as he ducked behind the red-tips flanking the back windows of Cora's unit. Using his handy tool kit, he jiggled open a window in seconds and slipped inside.

Just as he'd expected, the place was dark. Silent. It didn't smell of old people like he expected, not like that nursing home where his grandpa had been shoved for the last ten years of his sorry life.

Instead, the kitchen smelled like chocolate chip cookies as if the old broad had been baking. He thought she was in a wheelchair now, half crippled in her body and mind.

Inching past the oven, sure enough, he spotted the batch of cookies and snagged one, then wolfed it down, and grabbed another one and jammed it in his pocket.

Then moving slowly, he scanned the tiny apartment and tiptoed into the living room. The single bedroom was to the right. Inhaling a deep breath, he darted through the doorway as quiet as a mouse.

Cora was curled in bed, her white hair fanned across the pillow like Snow White. He stared at her for a moment, his Grandma Giselle's face flashing in his mind.

Dammit, he couldn't go soft now. The old biddy's own daughter had brought this on herself.

Gritting his teeth, he removed his phone from his pocket and texted Madelyn.

"I warned you to back off."

Then he slowly eased a pillow from the rocking chair beside Cora's bed and pressed it over her face.

Chapter Twelve

Madelyn's cell phone dinged, indicating she had a text. But the message on the screen made her pulse spike with fear.

I warned you to back off.

"Oh, my God…"

Caleb had just turned onto the main street of Sanctuary. "What's wrong?"

Panic rose in Madelyn's throat as she showed him the text. "What if he has Sara? Oh, God, oh, God, he warned me…" Tears blurred her vision.

"Don't panic. I just talked to Gage." Caleb grabbed his cell phone and punched Gage's number again. "It's Caleb. Is Sara all right?" A pause, then Caleb breathed out. "Good. Madelyn just received another text from the guy who threatened her before."

"Is Sara awake? If she is, let me speak to her," Madelyn pleaded. "Please. I need to hear her voice."

Caleb nodded. "Gage, if Sara is awake, put her on the phone. And watch out in case this guy tries something."

He handed the phone to Madelyn, and she gripped it with a shaky hand, unable to breathe for the few seconds it took for Gage to retrieve her daughter.

"Mommy," Sara said in a sleepy voice.

Relief nearly overwhelmed her. "Sara, baby, are you okay?"

"Yes. We're watching the movie—and Ruby likes to play dress up and paint, and we made Rudolph sandwiches with peanut butter and pretzels and raisins and a cherry for his nose."

Madelyn choked on a sob. Her daughter sounded so happy.

Caleb gently massaged her shoulder, and she took a deep breath.

"Mommy, what's wrong?" Sara asked as if she suddenly sensed Madelyn was upset. "Did you find Cissy?"

Oh, Lord, how was she going to answer Sara?

With the truth. That's all she could do. "Not yet, honey, but we're not giving up. Caleb and I are on our way to pick you up. We'll be there soon."

"'Kay. But Mommy, I likes Ruby so you don't gots to hurry."

Madelyn smiled, her heart finally calming as she heard the joy in her daughter's voice. Sara deserved to have friends and be normal, not plagued with worry or visions of murder.

Her cell phone jangled in her lap, and she checked the Caller ID. Sanctuary Seniors. "Grandma's calling, baby, let me talk to her and I'll see you in a bit."

"'Kay, Mommy. Love you."

"Love you, too." Madelyn clicked on the incoming one.

"Mrs. Andrews, this is security from Sanctuary Seniors. I'm sorry to have to call you this late, but there's been an incident."

Madelyn's blood ran cold. "What do you mean, an incident?"

"It's your mother," he said gruffly. "You should come over here."

"What happened?" Madelyn cried.

Instead of replying though, the phone went dead in her hand. Shuddering with fear, Madelyn gave Caleb a panicked look. The warning, the text...

Sara was safe. But the threat?

This maniac had gone after her mother....

MADELYN CLUTCHED CALEB'S ARM. "Caleb, go to my mom's complex. Hurry!"

Caleb's stomach roiled at the fear in her eyes. "Madelyn, what's wrong?"

"That was security at Sanctuary Seniors. Something's happened to Mom."

Caleb sped down the street leading to the seniors' community. He remembered the text message, and cold fear clenched his gut. The killer must have been watching. He knew Sara was being guarded, so he'd targeted the only other person in the world Madelyn cared about—her mother.

Frustration burned his gut. Dammit, who was this bastard? How could he be all over the place at once?

Because he wasn't working alone. First Nadine, then Howard and now Madelyn's mother… Someone was cleaning up the past and determined to keep them from finding Cissy.

Headlights glared from an oncoming vehicle, and he blinked his lights as a signal, but the car nearly skimmed his side and raced on.

Cursing, he spun the SUV into the parking lot of the seniors' home and screeched to a halt. But his mind remained on the car that had nearly run them off the road.

That driver could have been the killer leaving the scene.

Madelyn wrenched open the door and vaulted out at a dead run toward her mother's unit. Bright lights from the outside shot across the lawn like golden spikes. Afraid she might be walking into a trap, he dashed after her. If the killer had called instead of security and hadn't been in that car, he might be hiding out, waiting to ambush Madelyn.

"Madelyn, wait." He grabbed her arm. "Let me check first. If your mother was attacked, her attacker might still be here."

"But I have to go to her," she protested, yanking at his arm.

"Stop and think for a second." He massaged her shoulder. "Are you sure the caller was security? Did he give you his name?"

"No…he hung up before I could get it." Her gaze filled with terror as she realized his train of thought. "Oh, God, Caleb, what if he's hurt her?"

His pulse accelerated. He hoped to hell that wasn't the case. "Stay behind me."

Madelyn nodded and trailed him as they slowly walked up the sidewalk. If security had called, they would have phoned the police. But the police were nowhere in sight.

Caleb jiggled the front door and found it locked.

Madelyn dug in her purse. "I have a key." She handed it to him, and he unlocked the door, then threw up a warning hand urging her to pause for a moment.

A thump echoed from the bedroom, then a scream.

Caleb pulled a gun from inside his jacket, then scanned the dark interior, alert and posed in defense mode.

A low cry erupted from the bedroom this time, and Madelyn lunged toward the sound. But he pushed her behind him, and inched through the small living room. The window was open, cold air blowing in, chilling the room. The bedroom sat to the right of the hallway. Slowly they closed the distance to it.

But a board squeaked, and a gunshot zinged toward them. Madelyn screamed, and he shoved her down. "Stay low. I'm going after him."

Cocking his gun, he edged close to the wall and inched to the bedroom doorway. The man was leaning over Madelyn's mother, one hand shoving a pillow over her face while he aimed the gun at him.

Her mother was kicking and fighting, desperately trying to shove him off of her.

Caleb pointed his Glock at the attacker. "Let her go."

The man spun around, the mask over his face hiding his features.

"It's over," Caleb said. "Let her go and drop it."

They stared at each other for a long, tense moment, then suddenly the man released the pillow and vaulted through the window. Madelyn's mother wheezed and coughed, struggling for air.

He raced to her. "Are you all right?"

A sob erupted from her, but she gestured for him to go after the intruder. Madelyn raced to them.

"Call 911," Caleb shouted as he climbed through the window. He visually scanned the shadows for the culprit. Behind him, he heard Madelyn and her mother crying.

"Maddie?"

"I'm here, Mom," Madelyn whispered.

A shot zipped by Caleb's head, and he crouched to his knees taking cover by the corner of the building.

The back of the building was wooded, trees jutting up to the property with the units lined in a row, small yards and gardens separating them. Lights began flickering on in various homes, the residents obviously disturbed by the gunshots. Footsteps pounded to the left, and he headed in that direction.

A large courtyard sat to the left with walkways that wound through a garden and to a small man-made lake nestled by woods.

He spotted a shadow slinking through the maze and jogged toward it. Did the perp have a getaway vehicle stashed on a side road nearby?

A siren wailed in the distance, but Caleb saw the figure move again and followed him toward the wooded area. Then the man suddenly fled into the dense forest.

Squinting in the darkness, Caleb tried to see which direction he went, but the sound of a gun firing forced him to duck behind a tree. The bullet grazed his arm, and he cursed.

A second later, a car engine revved up. He ran after it and fired, but the son of a bitch had disappeared out of sight.

MADELYN'S PULSE THRUMMED with fear. Her mother was hysterical and breathing so hard she thought she might be having a heart attack.

"Mom, you're safe now." Madelyn gripped her mother's arms and forced her mother to look at her. The terror in her eyes was so stark it robbed Madelyn's breath.

"He… Someone was here," she cried. "He shoved a pillow over my face.…"

Madelyn hugged her mother close. If they'd been a few minutes later, her mother might not be here.

"I know, Mom. Caleb ran after him." They clung together, both crying for a moment, hanging on to each other for dear life.

Finally when her mother calmed, Madelyn pulled back to examine her. "Does your chest hurt, Mom?"

"No…no, I just couldn't breathe for a minute." She raised a shaky hand to her throat. "Why would some man try to kill me? I'm an old woman, I don't have anything valuable.…"

Guilt and anger suffused Madelyn. "I know, Mom. He attacked you to get at me." She swallowed hard and forced out the words. "I received a phone call warning me he'd hurt Sara if I didn't stop nosing around, but we left her with Caleb's friend, so he came after you instead."

Her mother's nails dug into Madelyn's arms. "What? Who threatened Sara?"

"I don't know his name," Madelyn said, shaking with fury. "But he knows I'm looking for Cissy and warned me to stop."

"You are not going to stop," her mother declared emphatically. "You're going to find Cissy and this maniac and put him in jail where he belongs."

"Mrs. Barker!" A loud pounding on the front door followed the shout, and Madelyn ran to the door. A security guard from the complex stood on the threshold, the sheriff on his heels along with an ambulance. "You called 911," the guard said. "What happened?"

Madelyn raked her hair back. "My mother was attacked tonight. The man escaped through the window, but Caleb ran after him."

"Where's your mother?" one of the medics asked.

She gestured toward the bedroom and the medics rushed to check on her. Madelyn crossed her arms in an attempt to hold her emotions at bay.

"Did you see your mother's attacker?" Sheriff Gray asked.

Madelyn shook her head. "Just his shadow, then he fired at me and Caleb."

"He had a gun?"

Madelyn nodded.

"Then we'll get a crime unit here. I also need to question your mother."

"Of course. She's shaken up, but I'm sure

she'll talk to you." Madelyn led him to the bedroom but stopped before they entered. "I think this may be the same man who killed Nadine Cotter and Howard Zimmerman. He called me and told me to stop investigating. Caleb and I left Sara with Gage McDermont. Then I got a call from some man claiming to be security saying that someone attacked my mother."

Sheriff Gray muttered something under his breath. "We should have your phone analyzed."

"Caleb already has one of his agents working on it."

Her mother was propped against the pillows now, her pallor slowly returning to normal, a stubborn gleam in her eyes. "I told these gentlemen that I'm fine."

"Her vitals are steady," one of the medics said. "But we can transport her to the hospital for observation overnight if you want."

"That's not necessary," Madelyn's mother said. But she absentmindedly rubbed at her neck, a sign that the ordeal had terrified her. "I'm just angry that that madman escaped."

Madelyn smiled at her mother. She might be partially paralyzed but she had spunk. "Mom, Sheriff Gray needs to ask you about the attack. Are you up to it?"

Her mother nodded. "Yes, of course."

The sheriff crossed the room and took the chair across from Madelyn's mother. "Mrs. Barker, tell me exactly what happened tonight."

Madelyn's mother cleared her throat, her look haunted. But anger flushed her cheeks, as well. A good sign. If she and Sara and Cissy had fight in them, Cora Barker was their inspiration.

"I was sleeping," she began. "Then suddenly the floor squeaked. That sound woke me. When I looked up, a big man was hovering over me. Then he shoved a pillow over my face and tried to smother me."

Sheriff Gray propped his hands on his knees. "Did you see the man's face?"

She fiddled with the sheet edge. "No, he wore a ski mask. One of those that cover your face."

"Did he say anything to you?" Sheriff Gray asked.

Madelyn's mother shook her head no.

"How about anything else distinctive? Did you notice an odor or hear another sound?"

Madelyn's mother closed her eyes for a moment and massaged her temple. When she opened her eyes, a frown marred her face. "Come to think of it, there was a smell. Some kind of oil, maybe cleaning oil or machine oil."

"Gun oil?" Sheriff Gray suggested.

Madelyn stiffened. Rayland Pedderson was a hunter. He had a shotgun that he'd aimed at them. And dozens of trophies on the walls of his lodge.

Had Pedderson attacked her mother?

CALEB CURSED AS HE JOGGED back to Cora Barker's apartment. Several neighbors peeped from behind curtains, curious about the commotion, but obviously too frightened to step outside. Had one of them witnessed something?

Thankfully the sheriff and a crime unit had arrived.

He stowed his weapon as he met Madelyn on the porch steps. She looked as if she was barely holding herself together. "Caleb, did you catch him?"

The sheriff appeared behind her, eyebrows raised.

"Afraid not." He scrubbed a hand through his hair. "He had a car waiting on the street."

"Did you get a look at him or the vehicle?" the sheriff asked.

Caleb shook his head. "No, it was too dark and far away to see the car. The perp was dressed in all black and wore a ski mask." He turned to Madelyn. "How's your mother?"

"Hanging in there," Madelyn said. "She

smelled some kind of oil on her attacker. It made me think of Rayland Pedderson. Could it be gun oil?"

Caleb frowned. "It's possible."

"Who is Pedderson?" Sheriff Gray asked.

Caleb filled him in. "He wasn't very happy to see us," Caleb said. "I'm sure he's hiding something."

"Adopted parents can become defensive when their adoptions are questioned," Sheriff Gray said. "I'm adopted myself so I can't say as I blame them."

"But we're not trying to tear their lives apart," Madelyn said. "We just want to find my daughter."

"You think Pedderson kidnapped your baby?" Sheriff Gray asked.

Madelyn shifted, jamming her hands in her jacket. "No, at least not from the photo of his family. But he might have information about the person who did."

"There's another couple we're looking for," Caleb admitted. "They go by the name Smith. When we tracked down their latest address, the place had been cleaned out. There were no signs indicating where they'd moved, either."

"I guess word has spread about Emery's adoptions being questionable and people are panicking. The adopted parents are afraid they'll lose their children," Sheriff Gray said. "Just raising that question could cause legal problems for the couples, as well as upset their families."

"It is a conundrum," Caleb agreed. "But Madelyn didn't give her daughter away, and if she's in danger, she needs us to save her."

"I'll check out Pedderson," Sheriff Gray agreed. "And this Smith couple. But first a crime unit needs to process your mother's room. Maybe the bullet casings will lead to something." He descended the steps to make the call, leaving the two of them alone on the porch.

Madelyn's gaze fell to Caleb's arm, then a horror-stricken expression crossed her face. "Caleb, you're hurt."

He glanced down at the rip in his shirt. A few drops of blood had seeped through the denim fabric. "It's just a flesh wound," he said shrugging it off.

Madelyn lifted his arm to examine it. Her adrenaline was waning, the worry in her eyes nagging at him. He wanted to wipe away that worry. Find her daughter and place her in Madelyn's arms.

Hell, he wanted to hold her so bad he ached.

She traced her fingers over his injury, leaning close to make sure he hadn't lied, that the bullet wasn't embedded in his arm. Her simple touch sent shards of sensations rippling through him.

He pressed his hand over hers. "It's nothing, I promise," he said, heat thrumming through him. When he'd chased after the shooter, he'd been terrified that the guy might have had an accomplice. That while he was distracted chasing one guy, another one would hurt Madelyn.

"Caleb," Madelyn whispered. "You should have the medics tend to this."

"I told you it's just a scratch. I'll clean it later." Her gaze locked with his, and need and desire heated his blood, hardening his body.

Desperate to touch her, to hold her, he feathered a strand of hair behind her ear. The temptation to kiss her seized him. He wanted to feel her against him, to know she was safe in his arms.

But voices inside interceded, jerking him back to reality, and he stepped away.

"I'm going to call Gage and have him post one of our agents with your mother."

Fear flashed in Madelyn's eyes for a moment, then gratitude. "Yes, please. Then I need to pick up Sara."

"Gage offered for her to spend the night."

"No," Madelyn said. "I need to see her. To have her home with me."

Caleb nodded. He understood that need. He felt the same way about being with her.

And that was crazy.

Madelyn was just a case to him.

But even as he phoned Gage and set up the guard, he knew he was lying to himself. Madelyn was not just a case.

He cared about her, dammit.

And that was dangerous.

Chapter Thirteen

Leaving her mother was difficult for Madelyn. But her mom assured Madelyn she was fine, then insisted that Madelyn be with Sara and continue the investigation.

Gage had sent Colt Mason over to guard her mother. He and Slade Blackburn planned to take shifts. Knowing they were guarding her mother helped alleviate the anxiety knotting Madelyn's shoulders as she and Caleb drove to Gage's.

But too many unanswered questions remained. The attacker was still free. People were dead. Cissy was missing.

Ben Camp had tried to trace the source of that text, but it turned out to be a dead lead. The message had come from a throwaway cell.

The sheriff had canvassed the neighbors to see if anyone had seen or heard anything, but with hearing impairments, poor vision, and the late hour, most of the seniors had only been aware something had happened when the sheriff and ambulance arrived.

Caleb was quiet on the drive, as well. In fact, he'd acted distant ever since she'd touched his arm and examined his wound. The big guy was definitely the silent type. Intense. Focused. Angry.

But she'd sensed his anger was triggered by the brute who had attacked her mother and escaped, not at her. That some part of him wanted her, at least on a primal level.

The same part of her that craved him.

The lights were still on at Gage's house when they arrived, and they hurried to the door together. Gage met them, his expression concerned.

"Are you all right, Madelyn?" Gage asked.

Madelyn nodded. "Thanks for assigning a guard to protect my mother. I don't know what I'd do if I lost her."

"We'll make sure that doesn't happen," Gage assured her.

Madelyn glanced over his shoulder. "Where are the girls?"

"They fell asleep watching a movie." They followed Gage through the foyer, and Madelyn spotted Ruby and Sara sprawled on a big, pink sleeping bag in front of the TV.

Leah looked up from the sofa with a smile. "Sara's an angel," she said softly. "The girls had a great time today."

"Thank you, I'm so grateful to you," Madelyn said, her emotions beginning to unfurl. "I'd be glad to return the favor sometime."

Leah stood, rubbing her lower back, then squeezed Madelyn's hands between hers. "Of course. I think we're all going to be good friends."

Madelyn nearly choked with gratitude. She hadn't realized how much she'd isolated herself since Tim had abandoned her. She'd been afraid of getting close to anyone, including another woman. But she was tired of being afraid. She and Sara both needed friends, a support group, as well as family.

Madelyn knelt to get Sara, but Caleb swooped her into his big arms instead. Sara stirred slightly, then curled against his broad chest, and Madelyn couldn't help but remember the connection her daughter shared with this man. She'd trusted him immediately.

Madelyn was so moved she couldn't speak. Caleb was tough and strong, protective and kind, and looked like an ancient Indian warrior. Yet he held her precious child more gently and with more care than Sara's father ever had.

The thought stayed with her while they drove back to her house.

"Let me check the house before you go inside," Caleb insisted as he pulled into the drive.

Reality made fear return, and she nodded, waiting in the Jeep until Caleb cleared the house. Thankfully, he returned and said it was safe. Then he carried Sara up to bed.

Sara stirred and looked up at her as Madelyn tucked her in bed. "Today was fun, Mommy. I like Ruby. Cissy will, too."

Madelyn dropped a kiss on Sara's cheek. "I love you, baby."

"I love you, too." Then Sara closed her eyes again and drifted back to sleep. Today had been harrowing. She'd nearly lost her mother.

And she couldn't lose her or Sara. Then she would be all alone.

She said a small prayer that Sara would rest tonight and be spared the nightmares.

But Sara's nightmares were the only real connection they had to her sister. And if Sara didn't dream of Cissy or see her in her sleep, she was terrified of what that meant.

That they were too late. That they'd never find her other daughter.

CALEB COULDN'T STOP THINKING about the fear on Madelyn's face when they'd heard her mother scream.

Or the way his body had tingled when Madelyn had touched him.

And then when he'd carried her daughter up the stairs, he'd seen the longing in Madelyn's eyes. She'd shut herself off from friends, from love, from relationships because she'd unselfishly been taking care of her daughter and her mother.

But who had taken care of Madelyn?

No one.

Her husband had deserted her. So had her father.

He would not desert her now.

Desperately trying to distract himself from wanting Madelyn, he studied her house. Homey, cozy furnishings. Comfortable, big club chairs draped with afghans that looked homemade. The fact that she owned a craft and hobby shop showed in the hand-painted folk art, stenciled walls and quilts in the room.

Her footsteps echoed as she descended the steps, and he jammed his hands in the pockets of his jacket, vying for control when he wanted to pull her into his arms and feel her up against him.

"Is she asleep?"

Madelyn nodded, then went to the corner cabinet and removed a wooden plaque. When she turned back, he saw that it was a nameplate with Cissy's name on it, one similar to the nameplate he'd seen hanging above Sara's bed. Both were painted with flowers in pinks and greens, their names decorated with swirls of color.

"You saved that all these years?" Caleb asked.

She nodded and hugged it to her chest. "I know we need to ask Sara about the secrets, but I couldn't bear to wake her."

"It's been a long day for all of us. We'll talk to her in the morning."

A relieved sigh escaped her, then she glanced at the nameplate again and a tear trickled down her cheek. "Thanks. I'm not sure how much more I could take today."

Her admission did it. He couldn't help himself.

He closed the distance between them in one stride, set the nameplate on the desk and pulled her up against him. "You're not alone, Madelyn," he whispered as she collapsed into his arms. "I'm here. Tonight you and Sara are safe."

"But what about Cissy?" she choked out.

Caleb closed his eyes, praying that Cissy was

safe, too. "Remember, she's strong. We'll find her. I promise."

God, take him from this earth if he broke that promise. Madelyn deserved to find her daughter. Sara deserved to have her twin.

And him… He didn't deserve to be holding her or to even entertain ideas of being a family with them, but he'd punished himself for so long that he sent up a second prayer. A prayer that Mara would understand. That she would want him to help Madelyn and her daughters.

That somehow God would give him the strength to perform a miracle and reunite the twins and their mother and catch the man who'd tried to kill Cora.

Madelyn's small body trembled against him, and he forgot about prayers and simply gave in to the need to comfort her. He stroked her back, rubbing circles between her shoulder blades, at the same time breathing in her sweet scent.

She made a soft sound of pleasure, and he savored the sound, nuzzling her hair with his face.

"Caleb, thank you for being here," she whispered.

He didn't want her thanks. He wanted her to want him. To crave him as much as he craved her.

"You don't need to thank me," he said gruffly. "I'm just doing my job."

She suddenly pulled away and dropped her hands, confusion and hurt mingling with the desire darkening her eyes. "I'm sorry, Caleb. You're right. You're just doing your job, and I'm being foolish, falling all over you."

Guilt hit him swift and hard. Desire and something primal and hot, something out of control, snapped inside him. Too many people had hurt Madelyn.

He couldn't allow her to think that he was rejecting her.

"It's not just my job," he said between gritted teeth because admitting his own needs cost him. "I want you, Madelyn. I want to help you, to protect you, to...hold you."

The truth of his words registered in her eyes and made them sparkle with desire and a hunger that mirrored the aching hole clawing at his gut.

Emboldened by that look, he yanked her up against him, angled his head and closed his mouth over hers.

She seemed stunned at first, and he ordered himself to move slowly, not to frighten her with his raging need for her. But it had been so long since he'd held a woman, desired a woman, that emotions and lust and hunger made him run his tongue along her lips, pushing, probing, begging to venture inside.

A low, throaty moan escaped her, and she leaned into him and tunneled her fingers through his hair and parted her lips. Then she whispered his name on a moan and sucked his tongue into her mouth.

The feel of her lips closing around his tongue sent white-hot heat blazing through his body. His bloodstream flooded with sensations, his sex going rock-hard.

She shifted her body against him as if she felt his thick length and ached for it, and he backed her against the wall, running his hands down the sides of her body until one hand cupped her breast and the other pressed her hips forward, planting her sex into the V of his thighs.

"Caleb…" She moaned again, dragged her mouth from his and sucked and nibbled at his neck.

"Madelyn," he whispered against her hair. His body ached for her.

He kneaded her breast, heaving for a breath as she slowly unbuttoned his shirt and dropped kisses along his chest and torso. When her head dipped lower, he cupped her face between his hands, lifted her face and stared into her eyes.

"You have to slow down or I'm not going to make it," he said with a wicked grin.

The sensuous look she returned nearly undid him. "I can't help it," Madelyn whispered. "I want you, Caleb. Like I've never wanted a man."

"I want you, too," he admitted. But dammit, he didn't have a condom. It had been so damn long that he had stopped carrying protection.

And he'd never take the chance of impregnating another woman. Not unless they were married and he knew she wanted his child.

His child...her child.

Guilt slammed into him. He couldn't screw up this case because of his own needs for Madelyn.

She deserved better.

"You changed your mind?" Madelyn said, hurt flashing in her eyes.

"No, I want you," he said, his voice gruff with desire. "But I want to do right by you even more."

MADELYN'S PULSE CLAMORED. Caleb wanted to do right by her.

But right now all she wanted was to have him kiss her again. To have him take her upstairs, strip her clothes and make love to her.

And she was going to have it.

"Please, Caleb," she whispered. "I need you tonight."

Questions filled his eyes. Then a flash of raw, primal need that took her breath away. She didn't know his story, but knew enough to realize that he didn't do this lightly. He was honorable, decent. He kept his promises.

And he was all man. She felt it in the thick, hard length between her thighs. In the control he maintained. In the heat flaring in his expression.

"Are you sure?" he asked gruffly.

She nodded.

"I don't have protection," he said with a frown.

Madelyn smiled. "I do." She blushed at the surprised look on his face. One of the times her mother had tried to fix her up, she'd given her a gift basket.

His mouth closed over hers again, gentle, then probing, then demanding, and she parted her lips and welcomed him inside. His tongue danced and teased her lips, played a game of tag with her own, then he suddenly swept her in his arms and carried her to her bedroom.

A sliver of moonlight flickered through the sheers illuminating his broad body, and her heart raced as he allowed her to remove his shirt. She ran her hands over his slick, smooth, bronzed chest, then flicked the leather thong from his hair and threaded her fingers through the decadent strands.

His gruff moan spurned her on and she nibbled and kissed and licked his neck and chest, until he grabbed her hands and pushed her back onto the bed. "My turn," he murmured as he began to strip her clothes.

"Condom?"

She gestured toward the decorative basket on her nightstand, and he chuckled. "You were prepared?"

"My mother," she said with a smile.

A sensual almost possessive look flared in his eyes, and he buried his head in her hair for a moment, as if savoring the way she felt in his arms. Madelyn felt a tenderness for him wash over her.

Then he lifted his head and a wicked gleam replaced that look, the raw, primal need in his eyes sending a buzz of euphoric anticipation through her as he began to peel off her clothes.

Madelyn hadn't been naked for anyone except her ex, and now she had a scar from the C-section. For a moment, she threw her hands down to cover it, but Caleb shook his head and flung her hands by her sides, holding them down as he ravaged her mouth again.

"You're beautiful," he growled. "I want to taste all of you."

Erotic sensations rippled through her as he swept his tongue down her neck, then he teased and nibbled and sucked her nipples into his mouth until she arched and cried out for more. She parted her legs, silently begging for him to fill her, but his tongue found its way down her belly and into her heat, and pure pleasure shot through her.

A million butterflies danced in her stomach as he kissed the insides of her thighs then tilted her hips to taste her.

"Caleb…"

Then she could speak no more. Her body became a minefield of sensations, exploding with each touch and caress, each kiss and lap of his tongue, and when she shouted his name as her orgasm claimed her, he rose above her, kissed her again, then plunged his huge length inside her.

CALEB SHIFTED, ALLOWING Madelyn to adjust to his size. She was so damn small and tight that he was afraid he would hurt her. But stopping now was out of the question. Her pleas for him to take her echoed in his head, the heat in his blood roaring.

Her body quivered around his sex, hugging him, holding him, then she wrapped her legs around him, and any rational thoughts fled. On some basic, male level, he had wanted her from the moment he'd seen her.

And it was destiny that he have her.

Her pain, her sweetness, her strength, her love for her family all made her sexy. And her body... She had the body of a vixen.

Tempting. Delicious. Sensual.

She clawed at his back, and his muscles rippled. She raked her feet down his calves and his sex hardened even more. She suckled his neck, and he rocked inside her, plunging to her core.

Need and desire and emotions he didn't want to name drove him faster, and he built a tempo that had his own climax teetering to the surface. Then she lowered her hands to grip his hips, and pleasure overcame him.

He stroked her inside and out, lifted her legs and sank deeper, so deep he felt another orgasm shivering through her. So deep his own came so swift and hard that he lost all thought and shouted her name as his body unloaded inside her.

MADELYN QUIVERED FROM the delicious sensations buzzing through her body. She had never been made love to like that, not with such force and need and...emotion.

She stroked his hair back from his forehead as he rolled them to their sides and cradled her against his chest.

She was falling in love with Caleb.

How stupid was she?

For a man, sex was sex. And she had practically begged Caleb for it. She couldn't become emotional and declare her feelings. She needed him to finish the investigation.

A sound from Sara's room startled her, then Sara's cry rent the air. She was having another nightmare.

Caleb heard it, too, and instantly released her. "You'd better check on her."

Madelyn nodded, her skin still tingling from his touch, her breasts heavy and aching. But she put aside her desires, grabbed a nightshirt from her dresser, yanked it on and rushed to her daughter.

Lost in the throes of another nightmare, Sara thrashed beneath the covers, a low sob ripping from her. "No, don't put me in there. It's dark...."

Madelyn sank down on the bed beside her

and shook her gently. "Wake up, sweetie. You're having another bad dream."

Sara cried out again, then opened her eyes. The glazed fear in her expression made Madelyn's stomach knot. "Sara, what did you see, baby?"

Sara stared at her for a heartbeat, the air vibrating with her terror. Behind her, Madelyn heard Caleb step to the door and realized he was watching. Listening. Waiting.

"What did you see?" Madelyn asked gently.

"Cissy," Sara said in a strained voice. "She's scared."

"Why is she scared, honey?"

"The mean man, he gots her and he dragged her away from the sunflowers."

Madelyn's gaze flew to Caleb's, and he slowly walked over to join them. He'd put on his jeans and shirt, although the shirt was half buttoned, reminding her of what they'd been doing. Making her want him again.

Making her feel guilty for indulging in pleasure when her daughters both needed her.

"Where are they now?" Caleb asked.

Sara tightened her fingers around the edge of her comforter. "He put her in the back of his car. But it's dark. She can't see anything."

"The back? You mean the backseat?" Caleb asked.

Sara shook her head. "No, the back where you puts stuff."

"You mean the trunk?" Madelyn said unable to keep the horror from her voice.

Sara bobbed her head up and down. "He slammed the top and closed Cissy in, and it's really dark and she's scared, and she's crying."

Madelyn shook with anger.

"What kind of car is he driving?" Caleb asked. "Can you see what color it is?"

Sara pressed her fist to her mouth. "Black."

"Does it have two doors or are there doors in the back?" Caleb asked.

Sara shrugged. "I don't know. Cissy can't see the doors. It's too dark in the trunk."

Madelyn ached for both of her girls. Apparently Sara saw everything through Cissy's eyes. And she felt her emotions. Her fear.

"Did the man say where he was taking Cissy?" Caleb asked.

Sara shook her head. "No, but the man killed her mama, and now he's taking her away."

Madelyn exchanged a worried look with Caleb. He knelt by Sara's bed. "Sara, you said once that Cissy shared her secrets with you. Can you tell us about those secrets?"

Sara's traumatized gaze flew to Caleb. "You're not supposed to tell each other's secrets."

Madelyn chewed her bottom lip, then gathered Sara's hand in hers. "You're right, honey. But Cissy's in trouble. And if there's something about her secrets that can help us find her, I don't think she'd mind if you told us."

"Your mom is right," Caleb said in a soothing tone.

Sara studied them both for a moment, indecision in her eyes. She was loyal to her twin, but she was terrified for Cissy's life. She clutched her teddy bear under one arm and clung to Madelyn's hand, squeezing it for dear life. "Cissy said no one's supposed to know."

"Know what, Sara?" Caleb asked.

Sara heaved a weary sigh. "That we gots the same daddy."

CISSY ROLLED INTO A BALL, hugging her blanket to her chest. Tears leaked from her eyes and dripped down her face. Her breath hitched. She'd screamed so much already that her throat hurt and her voice sounded like a frog.

But nobody had heard.

Unless Sara had....

The car bounced over the rough road, tossing her back and forth. It was so dark she couldn't see anything. It smelled awful, too. Dirty and greasy, and she felt a spider crawling up her leg.

She swiped at the spider with her hand and felt along the inside of the trunk for something to help her get out. But her hand hit something sharp. A shovel.

She jerked her hand back.

Her mommy's face flashed in her mind. Her mommy lying on the floor in all that red. The red was blood. Her mommy's blood cause the mean monster man had cut her throat.

The monster man had killed her. And now he'd left her mommy behind.

Where was he taking her now? To her daddy? Back to Sara?

No... He was going to kill her, too. That's why he had that shovel. He was going to kill her, then he would bury her in the ground and no one would ever find her.

And she would never get to be with Sara.

Chapter Fourteen

Madelyn's mind raced as Sara's words sank in.

Cissy knew that she shared a daddy with Sara. Had she actually met her father?

If that was the case, then her ex-husband knew that Cissy had survived. He might have even seen her. He might even know where she was.

Pain knifed through her. No… Tim would not have betrayed her like that. He couldn't be involved in Cissy's disappearance, in her adoption.

He wouldn't have given away one of his own children.…

Would he?

"Thank you for sharing with us." Caleb patted Sara's shoulder. "You're a brave little girl and a big help, Sara."

Panic mushroomed inside Madelyn. "Sara, is the mean man who hurt Cissy's mother—is that man Cissy's daddy?"

Sara scrunched her nose. "No... Her mama says it's her uncle. But he don't like Cissy. And he and Cissy's mama was yelling at each other and then...the knife..."

A horror-stricken look filled Sara's eyes again, and Madelyn pulled her into her arms. "It's okay, honey. It's over. We'll find Cissy. I promise."

Caleb stood, indicating his phone, then left the room as if he was on a mission. She laid down beside Sara and comforted her until she finally drifted back to sleep.

Madelyn closed her eyes, too, sleep pulling at her.

They had to find Tim.

And if he'd had any part in Cissy's adoption, she would kill him.

CALEB COULD BARELY CONTAIN his rage. Had Madelyn's husband sold their daughter?

And what was this about an uncle killing the mother?

He strode to Madelyn's kitchen table, the scent of her still lingering on his skin and tormenting him. Making love with her had been a mistake. He'd thought it would sate him, but now that he'd tasted her, touched her, felt her body join with his, he couldn't shake the need for her.

He checked his watch—too late to call Ben.

So he stretched out on the couch and closed his eyes. He dozed for a few hours, but woke with a start, adrenaline pumping through him. He retrieved his duffel bag from his car and hurriedly showered in the downstairs bath, not wanting to disturb Madelyn and Sara.

His mind spinning, he grabbed a pad and began to jot down the leads they had so far as he punched Ben's number.

"Hello. Camp here."

Caleb winced. Ben sounded half asleep.

"Ben, I'm sorry. I know it's early, but I think Madelyn's ex may have had something to do with her daughter's disappearance. Do you have a current address on him?"

"Hang on and let me pull up his file."

Caleb heard computer keys clicking, and continued to make his list, trying to pinpoint a connection. Emery had sold babies. Mansfield had helped arrange the adoptions.

Madelyn had a car accident—or had it been an accident?

Out of the couples who'd adopted through Emery, Pedderson was the most suspicious, and his beard matched Sara's description.

The last couple, the Smiths—probably a phony name—had disappeared, making them jump to the top of his suspect list.

Also, the two people who might have known that Cissy hadn't died had been murdered.

The killer was still at large. He'd sent Madelyn a threatening text and attacked her mother.

And he might not be working alone....

"Last address for Tim Andrews is a small town in the mountains of Tennessee," Ben said, interrupting his thoughts. "555 Trinity Lane, Bear's Landing."

Caleb jotted down the address, then Tim's name and drew a big question mark beside his name. "Anything else?"

Ben cleared his throat. "I ran his financials. Guy's in debt up to his eyeballs. He seems to have a pattern of big deposits, then equally large withdrawals. I'd say investments, but there's no evidence of a portfolio."

Son of a bitch. "Gambling," Caleb suggested.

"Sounds like it to me, too," Ben said.

Caleb glanced at the stairs, grateful Madelyn was still with Sara. "If the guy was in trouble five years ago, maybe he was desperate enough to sell his daughter to pay off his debt."

Ben whistled.

"Sara said something else disturbing. She said the man who killed her mother is her uncle." He paused. "See if any of the mothers or fathers on our list have brothers, then dig up everything you can on them. Maybe one of them has a police record or we'll find another connection."

"That'll take time, but I'm on it."

Caleb spotted one of Sara's sketches on the refrigerator. "Oh, and see if there are any greenhouses that specialize in sunflowers near Bear's Landing."

"Okay, hang on."

"I don't see any commercial greenhouses," Ben said a moment later. "That doesn't mean someone might not own a private one, but there are no wholesale ones in the area."

"It was a long shot," Caleb said, although he wanted to curse.

"Do you want me to ask Gage to send another agent to Andrews's place?"

"No," Caleb said. "I'm heading up there myself." He had a feeling Madelyn would insist on going, as well.

As much as he hated to put her through such an ordeal, they both needed to see her ex's face when they confronted him.

SUNLIGHT SHIMMERED THROUGH the blinds in Sara's room, but Madelyn had barely closed her eyes. Each time she did, images of her husband trading their baby for money taunted her.

She had to be wrong. Surely Tim wouldn't do something so horrible....

Madelyn slipped from bed and tiptoed to her room, then showered, closing her eyes and willing the images to fade, but they refused to go away.

She shampooed her hair, rinsed and dried off, then blew it dry and dressed in jeans and a loose sweater. She headed downstairs for coffee, wondering where Caleb was, if he'd slept on her sofa.

Their heated lovemaking the night before flashed back, and she inwardly groaned. That had been wonderful. Then Sara's cry had reminded her of the reason Caleb was there, that he'd be leaving as soon as they found her daughter.

The scent of coffee permeated the air, and Madelyn found Caleb in the kitchen with a mug, his face stony. No remnants of desire. No heated looks.

No good morning kiss or embrace or a hint that they would repeat it.

"Did you sleep?" he asked.

"Some." She poured herself a mug, aching to touch him again, but knowing she shouldn't. She had to put distance between them, couldn't let herself fantasize about a life with Caleb when she was certain the night before had only been sex for him. "You?"

He gave a nod. "I talked to Ben. I have an address for your ex. I'm heading to his place to talk to him."

Madelyn's stomach pitched, but she steeled herself. "Where is he?"

"A small town in the Smokies called Bear's Landing."

"I'm going with you."

Caleb didn't argue. He simply nodded. "I already talked to Gage. Leah and Ruby are expecting Sara."

Madelyn stared down into her coffee, tears threatening. "I'm going to owe her again."

"Leah and Gage are friends who want to help, Madelyn." Caleb placed both hands on her shoulders and massaged them. "So you don't owe anyone anything."

"I owed it to my daughters to protect them." She whirled around, anguish nearly suffocating her. "What if Tim did this, Caleb? What kind of mother am I if I didn't see what their father was capable of?"

"You are a wonderful mother," Caleb said gruffly. "And you trusted your husband. There's no crime in that."

Madelyn choked back a sob. "There is if he sold one of my children."

"We don't know that for sure," Caleb said. "But we are going to find out. Do you want me to get Sara?"

She sucked in a breath. "No, I need to get her dressed. While she has breakfast, I'll fill us some to-go mugs and we can take our coffee with us."

"Good idea. It's a long drive."

A half hour later, they drove to Leah's. "Did you have more bad dreams last night, Sara?" Caleb asked as he parked at Gage's.

She shook her head. "I think Cissy's sleeping."

He prayed the child was right, that her silence didn't mean something worse.

Madelyn walked Sara to the door, and Sara hugged her so tightly, Madelyn feared she wouldn't let her go. As much as she hated leaving Sara, she had to spare her the trauma ahead. Sara hadn't seen Tim in years; she wouldn't even recognize him. She certainly didn't need to watch her mother confront him with her suspicions.

"Come on, Sara," Ruby squealed. "Mommy made playdough for us!"

Sara smiled at Ruby and clasped her hand, then followed her to the kitchen.

Storm clouds gathered as Madelyn and Caleb left Sanctuary and headed toward Tennessee. Caleb concentrated on the road, and she concentrated on not falling apart.

Because with every mile that passed, her sense that Tim had lied to her and done the unspeakable mounted.

FOUR HOURS LATER, CALEB steered the Jeep up the winding road toward Bear's Landing. The sun had battled to make its way through the ominous clouds, the temperature dropping. Wind rattled trees, shaking leaves and sending them skittering to the ground, the shrill whistle of it roaring off the mountain like a siren screeching.

The small town of Bear's Landing was barely a blip on the map, a quaint little place with two stoplights, a couple of tourist shops, a diner and a gas station. A Native American reservation bordered the town with signs offering handmade crafts. Signs for a fishing lodge, waterfalls and camping pointed to a dirt road; another sign indicated a group of log homes built along the creek running along the mountain.

Madelyn gazed out the window, but he sensed

she wasn't looking at the scenery, that she was contemplating what her husband might have done.

He spotted a sign for a place called Hog's Valley, then Trinity Lane, and turned left, then followed it along the creek. The graveled road ended at a split-level log house surrounded by natural woods. A deer grazed in the field to the side, the creek rippling behind the property.

Caleb scanned the drive and surrounding property in search of Andrews, his vehicle, even toys indicating that Tim might have actually taken custody of Cissy himself.

A shiny black pickup sat adjacent to the house. But he saw no sign of the man or any evidence of a child.

"This is where Tim lives?" Madelyn asked surprised.

"It's the address Ben gave me."

"Odd. Tim never seemed like the outdoors type." She reached for the door handle. "Then again, I obviously didn't know my husband at all, did I?"

"Some people are masters of deception," he said, hating the self-recriminations in her tone.

Instincts kicking in, Caleb checked his weapon as he exited the Jeep, then took Madelyn's arm.

"We have to be careful. If he's on to us, he might be armed and dangerous."

"I wish I had that gun we talked about," Madelyn said. "I'd show him dangerous."

A tiny smile quirked at the corners of Caleb's mouth. He didn't blame her.

They slowly made their way up to the door, the wind beating at the porch rocking chair and sending it swinging back and forth as if a ghost was sitting in it. Dead ferns hung from the rail as if long forgotten, an empty beer can was tipped on its side by a hammock, a newspaper rattled in the breeze.

The paper was an old issue—the front-page story featuring the arrest of Dr. Emery. That event had obviously triggered panic among those involved in the illegal adoptions. Everyone had been scrambling to cover their butts.

And Nadine and Zimmerman were dead because of it.

Madelyn exhaled beside him, and he squeezed her arm, silently offering encouragement. He opened the screen door, then rapped the bear-paw door knocker.

Shadows from the storm clouds darkened the porch, the wind pounding the roof.

Caleb knocked again, then wielded his gun at the ready as he turned the knob. The door was locked so he removed a clip from his pocket and picked the lock.

The door swung open with a screech. He threw up a hand, silently commanding Madelyn to stay behind him.

Slowly he inched inside the house. The rooms were dark, the sound of a clock ticking in the silence. He scanned the foyer, then moved toward the open room spanning the back of the house, a large den with a stone fireplace that adjoined the kitchen. All rustic decor. A plain, beige rug. Brown sofa. Cheap paintings of deer and wildlife. A barrel-shaped lamp had been knocked on the floor, magazines scattered, another wooden chair overturned as if there had been some kind of trouble.

Caleb eased through the room, careful not to touch anything, then spotted a dark reddish-brown stain on the braided rug beneath the oak table.

A stain that looked like blood.

Dammit.

"Stay here, Madelyn. I'm going to check upstairs."

He hoped to hell he found Andrews alive so they could get some answers. Then he could have the pleasure of killing him.

But that blood wasn't a good sign. Tim Andrews might already be dead.

If he was, then who in the hell was behind all the murders?

MADELYN SHUDDERED AS SHE glanced across the room. Something bad had happened here. A fight.

Where was Tim?

Her gaze swept across the overturned chair, the broken lamp, then the bare furnishings, the lack of personal touches, the lack of warmth, and she realized Tim hadn't made a home here.

The cheap watercolors on the walls were probably from a discount store. There were no videos or CD's, no comfortable throw pillows, no sign of the man she'd known.

Except for the one framed photo on the mantle. Sara.

Had he been watching them?

She picked up the photograph, zeroing in on the details. Sara wore a red bathing suit, and she was standing in front of a kiddie pool in the backyard, her hair in pigtails.

Her breath caught.

Except Sara didn't have a red bathing suit. And that yard was not Madelyn's.

Her throat flooded with nausea and happiness and shock.

It wasn't Sara.

This was a picture of Cissy. The little girl she'd lost. The baby her husband had told her had died.

The extent of Tim's betrayal hit her like a fist in the gut. She doubled over, the pain and grief so intense her legs buckled and she collapsed on the floor, hugging the picture to her.

Tim had known where Cissy was all this time and hadn't told her....

Chapter Fifteen

Caleb recognized the signs of a bachelor living in the house. No personal items. No warmth of a woman's touch. Basic black comforter and lack of pictures on the walls upstairs. There was also a desolate, lonely feel to the place as if it had been a self-imposed prison of sorts.

You should have been locked in a damn cell for what you've done, Andrews.

He quickly surveyed the two bedrooms and found them empty, the master bed unmade. But there was no blood or signs of a struggle upstairs.

He glanced around for a computer, hoping to glean information from it, but didn't find one. He dug in the man's dresser drawers searching for notes, a secret file, but came up empty, as well.

Suddenly a heart-wrenching sob echoed from downstairs, then another, and Caleb's heart constricted.

Madelyn.

Forgetting all else but her, he stormed down the steps. When he saw her kneeling on the floor, her anguish seeped into his soul.

Dear God, had she found something? Evidence that Cissy was dead?

Fear clawed at him as he slowly approached her. He stooped down to her level, terrified what that photo might reveal. Gently he stroked her arms, then pulled her to him, rocking her back and forth and rubbing slow circles around her back while she sobbed.

Several tense minutes passed while she purged her emotions, but he waited until her crying subsided before he spoke.

"Madelyn, honey, I'm so sorry," he said gruffly. "Talk to me. Tell me what's wrong."

Dragging in a cleansing breath, she lifted her face and showed him the photo. "It's Cissy," she whispered raggedly. "Not Sara. This is Cissy and it was taken recently."

Which meant that her damn husband had not only known her daughter had survived, but he'd known where she was all along.

His gaze flew toward the blood on the floor. So where was the bastard now?

Madelyn suddenly raced over to the built-in

bookcases, flung open the doors and began to search inside.

"What are you doing?" Caleb asked.

"Looking for more pictures, a scrapbook, an address. Something that will give us a clue as to where Cissy and her adopted mother live." She heaved a breath. "Did you find anything upstairs?"

"No. No computer. Nothing about Cissy."

Caleb's phone jangled, so he connected the call.

"Caleb, it's Gage. Have you made it to Andrews's place?"

"Yeah. But he's not here, and I found blood." Caleb released a frustrated sigh, then lowered his voice. "Madelyn also found a photo of Cissy."

"She's alive?"

He angled his body away from Madelyn. "She was in the picture, and it looks as if it was taken recently."

Gage emitted a long-winded sigh. "He deserves to rot for this."

"I agree. Can you have the sheriff issue an APB for Andrews? And send word to the Tennessee authorities, too."

"I'll do it as soon as we hang up."

"Is Sara all right?"

"Yes, but I'm here with Ben, and we're on speakerphone. We may have a lead."

"Thank God. We need one. Did Brianna find something on the adoptions or through DFAS?"

"No, but Ben accessed incoming police reports and there's been a murder not too far from Bear's Landing. Woman with her throat slashed."

Caleb's adrenaline kicked in. "Did she have a child?"

"Yes, a daughter. Police report said they identified the woman as Danielle Smith."

"We were hunting for the Smiths." Caleb clicked his teeth. "What about the child?"

"No sign of her at the house. But I figured you'd want to check it out."

"Definitely." Caleb reached in his pocket for a pen and a notepad, then scribbled down the address. "Now see if you can find out the Smiths' real name. I think the woman's brother may be responsible for her death."

"I'm on it," Ben said. "Let us know what you find at the Smith house."

"Right." Caleb disconnected the call. "Madelyn," he said in a quiet tone.

She whirled around, then flung out her hands. "There's nothing else here. No photo albums. No letters or signs of where she is." She gestured toward the framed photo. "Why would he have that photo and nothing more?"

"I don't know," Caleb said honestly. "There's a lot I don't understand about your ex. Why he left you. How he could have abandoned his children."

Hurt flickered in her eyes. "I can't believe he knew where Cissy was all these years and let me believe she was dead."

Caleb moved toward her, wanting to comfort her, yet they didn't have time. He had a lead and they needed to act upon it. "He'll pay. I promise, Madelyn." He gently took her face and cupped it between his hands. "I know you're hurting, but Gage phoned. There's been a murder, a woman killed, not too far from here. We need to go."

"Oh, God, you think it's Cissy's adopted mother?"

"It's possible." He coaxed her toward the door. "Police said her name is Danielle Smith."

"Did they find a child?"

He shook his head. "No. The woman had a little girl, but she wasn't at the house."

Still there might be evidence confirming that this Smith woman had adopted Cissy. And some lead as to where the killer had taken her.

FEAR AND SHOCK SETTLED over Madelyn but she forced her mind to turn itself off. The horrible scenarios bombarding her were too painful to bear.

Caleb raced around the mountain, cutting through side roads and speeding around curves. The short drive felt like hours.

Ten minutes. Tim had lived *ten* damn minutes from their daughter and never told her. He'd watched Cissy grow up.

Had he shared birthdays with her and this woman? Had she called him Daddy?

And what had they told Cissy about her? Did Cissy think she had given her away?

She balled her hands into fists in her lap as they turned up a drive and climbed a hill which leveled off to an acre at the top offering a majestic view of the mountain. Two police cars were parked in front of the house, an ambulance and a black sedan beside them.

A white two-story house sat on the edge of the ridge, but to the left Madelyn spotted a greenhouse.

Her breath quickened. The sunflower greenhouse Sara had seen through Cissy. "This is it, Caleb. This is where Cissy has been living."

Caleb reached for his door handle. "Wait here. I'll talk to the sheriff."

"No way." Madelyn leaped from the Jeep and jogged up the hill to the house, but Caleb caught up with her.

"Remember, Madelyn, this woman has been murdered. The police are going to be suspicious of everyone until they catch the killer, so watch what you say."

Madelyn froze and stared at him, her lungs tightening. "You mean they'll think I killed her?"

"You have motive," he said in a low voice. "But thankfully, I can alibi you. Still, be careful."

Madelyn nodded, swallowing back a protest, then walked with Caleb to the front door. The uniformed officer guarding the entrance narrowed his eyes at them. "Deputy Holbrook," the man said. "Who are you and what are you doing here?"

Caleb flashed his ID. "I'm an investigator with GAI in Sanctuary, North Carolina, and we're looking into a missing child case," he explained. "Sheriff Gray is aware of our investigation and notified us there was a murder here. We believe the victim may be related to our case."

"Did you know the victim?" Deputy Holbrook asked.

"Not personally," Caleb said. "We think she may have adopted Mrs. Andrews's daughter."

The deputy spoke into his mike. "Sheriff, there's a couple here demanding to speak to you."

Voices from the back indicated the police, crime scene techs and probably a medical examiner were consulting, then footsteps sounded and a short, stocky man with wavy, brown hair appeared.

"Sheriff Dwight Haynes," the man said, looking back and forth between the two of them.

"Caleb Walker from GAI in Sanctuary, North Carolina, and this is Madelyn Andrews."

"What are you doing in Tennessee?"

Caleb explained about Cissy's disappearance. "I'm sure you're aware that a doctor at Sanctuary Hospital was arrested for kidnapping and arranging illegal adoptions?"

Sheriff Haynes nodded. "Yeah, I heard about the case."

"Mrs. Andrews was told that her baby died at birth," Caleb continued. "But recently we've uncovered evidence indicating she's alive, and we think your victim adopted her. She also might have been an accomplice in the baby's kidnapping."

The sheriff narrowed his eyes. "What led you to believe that?"

Caleb explained about Nadine Cotter's and

Howard Zimmerman's deaths, the connection between phone calls, then the link with Madelyn's ex-husband.

Madelyn stood on tiptoe, struggling to see past the deputy and sheriff to the inside of the foyer. She wanted pictures, proof, anything to confirm that Cissy had actually lived in this house. She was starved to know what her life had been like, if she had friends, if she was… loved.

"Interesting story," the sheriff said. "We'll let you know what we find here."

Caleb refused to be dismissed so easily. "The victim's name was Danielle Smith, correct?"

Sheriff Haynes nodded.

"Smith was the name of one of the adopted couples on the list we're investigating."

"If you'd just let us look around," Madelyn cut in. "Maybe there are pictures of this woman and my daughter that will prove our theory."

"If you lost her when she was born, how would you even know what she looked like?" Haynes asked.

"She was an identical twin," Madelyn said, irritated. "Please, I think she may be in danger. I need to know if she was here."

"This is a crime scene," the sheriff said. "I'm sorry, but I can't allow you inside."

"Listen to me," Madelyn said, desperation tingeing her voice. "My other daughter Sara has a connection with her sister. She saw this woman being murdered."

"You're telling me that your child witnessed Ms. Smith's murder?" Sheriff Haynes asked sharply. "If so, where is she? We need to question her."

Perspiration beaded on Madelyn's neck. "She wasn't here at the time. I told you they have a connection, a psychic, twin connection," Madelyn said, then quickly realized by the skeptical expression on his face that he didn't believe her.

Instead he gave her a dismissive look, then addressed Caleb. "Mr. Walker, I suggest you take your client and leave. I'm investigating a murder, and I don't have time for these games." With that curt statement, he turned around and walked away.

"He has to let us in," Madelyn said, ready to plow her way through.

But Caleb pulled her back from the doorway. She pushed at him, but he gently grabbed her hands and urged her down the stairs. "We'll come back when they're gone, Madelyn. Then we'll search the inside. I promise."

Still Madelyn's heart ached and panic clawed

at her as he escorted her to the Jeep. If Sara was right and the killer had put Cissy in the trunk of his car, there was no telling where he was now or what he intended to do with her.

Every second counted.

SARA PLUNGED HER PAINTBRUSH into the brown paint. Ruby was painting a beautiful sunset in red and yellow and orange.

But Sara's vision blurred, and suddenly she saw Cissy crying.

"Sara, I don't like it here."

"Where are you, Cissy?"

"I don't know. It's dark," she whispered.

Sara gripped the paintbrush tighter. "Tell me, so I can find you."

"He dragged me from the trunk into this old cabin," Cissy whispered. "But I can't move 'cause he tied me in the closet." She sniffled. "But I saw an old well house outside."

Sara's hand began to move, drawing a picture of the old wooden house. She closed her eyes for a minute, then she was in Cissy's mind. She saw the house, the dirty floor, the woods, the old well house.

There were long buildings on the hill beside the house, too. Long and narrow. Three of them. And they smelled like…poop.

Her hand shook as she opened her eyes and began to give them shape on the canvas.

Ruby walked over and looked at her painting. "That's good, Sara. Those must be chicken houses."

Sara added a wooden sign with a rooster etched on it. "It's where the mean man has my sister." She turned and ran to the kitchen. "Miss Leah, Miss Leah."

Leah stooped down and patted her shoulder. "What is it, honey?"

"I gots to call Mommy and Mr. Firewalker and tell them where Cissy is."

Chapter Sixteen

Caleb drove to the small diner in town and ordered a late lunch, hoping the crime unit would finish with the house by the time they were done. Although truthfully it might take hours before they finished processing the place.

He scarfed down two burgers, but Madelyn barely touched her turkey sandwich. Her gaunt face disturbed him. "You should try to eat something to keep up your strength."

"I can't think about food." She traced a drop of water from her tea glass then glanced out the window at the snow that had started to fall. "Just look at the weather. It's getting colder, and the weatherman is predicting a blizzard."

Caleb covered her hand with his, searching for words to console her, but his cell phone buzzed. He checked the caller ID. Gage's home phone.

He quickly punched Connect. "Caleb speaking."

"Caleb, it's Leah. Sara needs to speak to her mother."

"Is everything okay?"

Madelyn tensed across from him, and he squeezed her hand.

"Yes, but she saw Cissy again and she needs to tell you where she is."

A sliver of alarm ran up Caleb's spine. "Put her on the phone."

A second later, Sara's tiny voice echoed over the line. "Mr. Firewalker?"

"Yes, Sara. Miss Leah said that you know where Cissy is."

Madelyn's eyes widened, and she gestured for him to hand her the phone, but he held up a finger silently asking her to wait.

"She's in an old cabin, but he tied her in the closet." Tears laced Sara's voice.

Damn. He forced himself not to react so as not to frighten Madelyn.

"Can you tell me more about the cabin?"

"There's a well house outside." Sara sniffled loudly. "And three chicken houses that smell like poop and a wood sign."

"That's good, Sara," Caleb said. "Anything else?"

"The sign has a picture of a rooster on it."

He frowned. Maybe it was an old chicken farm. Probably an abandoned one.

"Anything else, honey?"

Sara's shaky breath echoed back. "No. Does that help, Mr. Firewalker? Can you find Cissy now?"

"That is a huge help," Caleb assured her. "If you think of anything more, ask Miss Leah to call back."

"'Kay."

"Let me speak to her," Madelyn insisted.

"Sara, I'm going to have your mommy call back on her phone. I need to use mine to call my friends so we can track down those chicken houses."

He said goodbye, then looked up at Madelyn. "Sara described an old house with a well and chicken houses. Maybe Ben can search maps of the area and we can pinpoint a location."

He tossed some cash on the table to pay the bill, punching Ben's number as he strode toward the door. Madelyn hurried after him, dialing Sara.

"I'll start searching now," Ben said after Caleb had caught him up-to-date.

Caleb opened the door and let Madelyn go through, then they rushed through the snow to his Jeep. "Thanks. We're going back to the

Smith woman's house to see if we can get inside this time. Maybe we'll find a lead there."

The snow began to thicken as he cranked the Jeep and drove from the diner, the wind howling. Madelyn was talking to Sara in a low voice, praising her for her help.

Unease settled in his gut. With the blizzard threatening and visibility poor, tracking anyone through the mountains was going to be nearly impossible.

But there was a little girl out there missing, a terrified little girl tied in a dark closet somewhere who needed him.

And nothing was going to stop him from finding her.

MADELYN STARED AT THE snowstorm outside as the Jeep ate the miles to the Smith house, her heart thundering. What if this madman left Cissy out there in this cold?

No, she couldn't think like that. They'd come this far. They were going to find her.

Thankfully, the police and crime units had dispersed by the time they reached the house. She assumed the woman's body had been transported to the morgue for an autopsy.

"Where was Danielle Smith's husband?"

Caleb shrugged. "Good question. Maybe we'll

find that answer as well as a clue to the killer's identity inside."

Caleb removed latex gloves again and shoved a pair in Madelyn's hands. "We're not supposed to be here, so wear these."

Nerves knotted her stomach as she stared at the yellow crime scene tape and signs warning them not to enter. Caleb motioned for her to follow him around back, and he found a window that wasn't locked. He climbed through it, then rushed and opened the back door for her.

Bile flooded her throat when she spotted the dark crimson stain on the white tile floor. There were also blood splatters on the sink and wall, the smell nauseating.

"Don't think about it," Caleb said matter-of-factly. "We need to hurry, Madelyn. Just look for notes, addresses, something that might tie the Smith woman to the adoptions."

But Madelyn barely heard him. Her gaze was fixed to the refrigerator where a crude child's drawing hung by a magnet. A drawing of twin blonde girls holding hands dancing in the midst of a sea of sunflowers.

A strangled sob caught in her throat, and she raced over and snatched it. "God, Caleb, look. This is just like Sara's drawing."

Caleb's eyes widened, the realization that

Cissy had lived here, that her connection with Sara was real, was undeniable.

Spurred by the sketch, Madelyn's adrenaline kicked in. She needed more, to see pictures of her lost child. To see what she'd been doing, what her life was like.

To see if Tim had been part of it.

Caleb began searching the kitchen desk and she took the drawers, racing from one to the other, hastily pushing through bills and grocery lists and random items. She found other drawings Cissy had made, some depicting herself alone, at the park, some with a woman who must have been Danielle Smith.

But none with her father.

Frantic for more, she rushed into the living area and scanned the room. Photos of Cissy chronicling her growth from infancy to present-day filled the wall. Tears burned Madelyn's throat as she saw the years of her missing daughter's life laid out in front of her. Cissy cradled in a pink blanket shortly after birth. Cissy learning to crawl. Her first step. Playing in the laundry basket. Splashing in a baby pool. Blowing bubbles in the bathtub. Learning to ride a tricycle.

Christmases and birthdays and other holidays—all photographed and honored, all ones she had missed.

The pain threatened to bring her to her knees. But she found something in those photos to hang on to, something to stop her from collapsing with utter grief. The young woman who had adopted Cissy looked at her with such love and adoration that Madelyn's heart swelled with gratitude.

Gratitude and anger.

That should have been her holding Cissy, feeding her, teaching her to ride a trike. Sharing birthdays and holidays and watching her play and grow with her twin.

Had Danielle Smith known she had robbed Cissy's birth mother of those treasured moments? Or had she been innocent? Simply a woman wanting a child and getting caught up in an adoption scheme she knew nothing about?

Caleb's voice jerked her from her emotional tirade. "Did you find anything?"

She gestured toward the photographs unable to speak.

A muscle ticked in Caleb's jaw as he scanned the wall of memories.

"Danielle's husband was killed in Iraq while they were waiting to adopt." Caleb showed her a photo he'd found in the kitchen desk. "Apparently he received an award. Died a hero."

And Danielle—had she died protecting Cissy?

"Madelyn, come on. I found a crude map I think the killer might have dropped. It could lead us to where he took Cissy."

Madelyn choked back the tears and took a deep breath. "Then let's go. Danielle Smith may have loved Cissy, but we're all my little girl has now."

CALEB WAS ON THE PHONE the moment they stepped out the door. "Ben, Gage, I found a map at the Smiths' house." He described the details to them and waited while Ben cross-checked it with the topographical maps online.

"There is an abandoned chicken farm near where you're describing," Ben said, then gave him the coordinates. "Used to be called Rooster's."

"We're heading there now," Caleb said as he and Madelyn jogged to the Jeep and jumped in.

Caleb ended the call, then tore away from the house, gravel and snow spewing behind his wheels as he careened down the driveway.

"Do you know where this place is?" Madelyn asked.

"I know the general area," Caleb said. "We may have to park and hike in on foot."

Although the storm was growing thicker,

the windchill dangerous. And the killer was armed.

Visibility was poor, slowing him down on the road, and tension thrummed in the car as he maneuvered along the mountain road. A half hour later, he found the turnoff. He veered left, then cursed as he spotted a fallen tree blocking the road.

"Dammit. We'll have to go on foot from here."

Madelyn buttoned her coat and yanked on a hat and gloves she retrieved from her pocket. "Then let's go."

Caleb tugged on gloves himself, then climbed out, checked to make sure he had an extra clip for his gun, then took Madelyn's hand and they began to hike. The storm swirled snow and leaves and twigs around them, branches breaking off as the blizzard gained momentum.

Trees swayed with the downfall, the snow so thick that their boots sank in the slush, but they continued to trudge, Caleb using his instincts to follow the road. Madelyn shivered, and he pulled her against him, helping her over stumps and through the thick slush. Animal life scurried for cover and to seek protection while the sun disappeared into the haze of white.

"What if she's out here?" Madelyn shouted over the roar of the wind.

"Sara said she was inside the house." He purposefully omitted the part about her being tied up in the closet fearing that would send Madelyn over the edge. And he needed her to be strong now.

Three miles in, and the storm intensified. Ahead, he spotted a cave and guided Madelyn to it. Maybe she could wait inside.

But a gunshot suddenly rent the air, skating near their heads. Madelyn screamed, and he grabbed her hand and ran toward the cave. Another bullet zinged toward them and Caleb shoved Madelyn down, crouching low as he tried to usher her to safety.

Just as they reached the cave and Madelyn ducked inside, someone jumped Caleb from behind. He felt a hard whack on his head, then struggled with the man, but his attacker slammed the butt of the gun against his head and stars spun in front of Caleb's eyes.

He must have blacked out because when he roused a moment later, he was lying in the snow, blood dripping in his eyes.

And a bearded man was holding a gun to Madelyn's head.

Chapter Seventeen

Sheer terror seized Madelyn as Rayland Pedderson jammed the barrel of his gun into her temple. His fingers tightened around her neck, his grip steely and locking her body against his. The urge to kick and bite and fight him shot through her.

But one wrong move, and she would be dead.

Then her girls would be alone, with no one to love and care for them.

Forcing herself to remain calm took every ounce of restraint she possessed.

When she'd noticed the blood running down Caleb's head, she was terrified he was dead.

And she'd realized she really did love him. Heart-pounding, soul-deep love that could last a lifetime. What if she never got to tell him?

"You bitch, you couldn't leave it alone, could you?" Pedderson growled near her ear.

"No," Madelyn said between gritted teeth.

"Cissy is my little girl. Why did you take her?"

"My sister wanted a child and you had two," he hissed. "Your husband thought you'd get over it and be happy with the baby you had."

The pain of Tim's betrayal knifed through her again. "But why did Tim sell our little girl?"

His fingers dug into her throat as he tried to drag her toward the woods. Snow pelted them, the brittle wind biting at her face. "Because the damn fool owed me money for some property he bought. Thought he'd develop it into some condos and make a fortune. But he spent that money gambling and owed me and his bookie. Hell, it was your damn husband who thought up the idea of sideswiping you to make you go into labor."

Madelyn had thought she couldn't be shocked anymore, but the realization that Tim had purposely been a part of her accident made her head reel.

At least Danielle's husband had died with honor. But Tim… "He sold our little girl for cash to pay off gambling debts?" Madelyn cried. "I'm going to kill him."

"Don't worry, I took care of him myself. He panicked in the end and wanted to call you. He even tried to get the girl back."

Tim was dead? She should be relieved, but she felt robbed of the chance to vent her anger and bitterness toward him.

"But Danielle was your sister. How could you kill her?" Madelyn asked, putting the pieces together in her mind.

"Damn idiot woman found out how we got Cissy and wanted to contact you. Said that little girl was psychic or something, that she kept talking about her twin. I warned her if she called you, she'd lose her kid."

Tears blurred Madelyn's eyes, trickling down and freezing on her cheeks. Poor Danielle. She'd obviously loved Cissy, but she'd still planned to do the right thing. Sara and Cissy were right. This man was a monster.

"Where's Cissy?" Madelyn asked. "Please let me have her back, and you can disappear. I don't care. I just want my daughter back."

"You hired a damn P.I.," Pedderson growled. "It's too late to make a deal."

"Please don't hurt Cissy," Madelyn pleaded. "She's just a child."

"I warned you," he mumbled, then a click sounded as he cocked the trigger. He was going to shoot her in cold blood.

A second later, a gunshot echoed, and she felt herself falling.

Falling, falling, falling…

Pedderson collapsed on her, blood soaking her shirt, his weight trapping her.

It took her a moment to realize she hadn't been shot.

Pedderson had.

Sobbing with relief, she shoved at his chest, desperate to move him off her.

"Madelyn!" Then suddenly Caleb was there, yanking at Pedderson's beefy body.

"Madelyn, are you hit?"

He dragged the heavy man off her, then shoved his body to the side. Blood pooled from his chest, his eyes were open stark wide, his body limp.

She should feel pity, but she felt nothing for the man except a cold rage. Caleb had shot him straight in the heart.

"Are you hurt?" Caleb raked his hands over her arms and legs and body, searching for injuries.

She shook her head, still in shock, then he hugged her against his chest.

"Dammit. I thought I'd lost you." His voice was hoarse with emotion, his hands soothing. She didn't realize she was crying until he pulled back and wiped her cheeks with his thumbs.

"Tim sold Cissy to him for money," she said,

choking on the words. "He sold our baby to pay off gambling debts."

He cradled her face between his hands. "I heard everything. I'm so sorry, Madelyn."

Tears streamed down her face. Snow pelted them. Blood was clotting in Caleb's hair, and she reached up to feel his wound, but he pushed her hand away.

"I'm fine. We have to find Cissy."

Panic threatened to immobilize her. "If she's out here alone, she'll never survive."

Determination hardened Caleb's face. "Sara said she's in a cabin," he said. "We'll follow Pedderson's tracks."

A surge of adrenaline shot through Madelyn, and she pushed to her feet. "Then let's go. We can't waste a minute."

CALEB LED MADELYN THROUGH the woods, tracking Pedderson, although the snow was making it almost impossible to move quickly or spot his footfalls. But he had the GPS coordinates and an innate sense of direction that guided him along the way.

"Look over there!" Madelyn tugged away from him and ran toward a tree stump. He jogged after her and caught up with her just as she lifted a pink blanket from the ground.

"This is Cissy's," Madelyn cried. "She was holding it in one of the pictures."

"Let me hold the blanket for a moment." Caleb reached for the blanket. "Maybe I can get a vision from it." Madelyn shoved it in his hands, and he closed his eyes and concentrated, but nothing came. Cissy's connection was with her sister, not with him. He needed Sara here, but bringing her out in this storm would be crazy. Choppers would never make it.

They were on their own.

He grabbed Madelyn's hand. "Come on, I think the cabin's close to here." Caleb pointed to the right.

Madelyn tucked the blanket beneath her arm, and they slogged through the snow, running as fast as they could. Wind and snow pummeled them, but they climbed over tree stumps and wove through the woods following the stream until they spotted a small, brown structure nestled on the hill.

"There it is!" Caleb shouted over the howling wind.

Together they ran toward the cabin, heaving for breath as they stumbled to the entrance. Caleb shoved at the door and entered first, still on guard in case Pedderson had had an accomplice.

Madelyn froze, her body going rigid. "Tim, you rotten, lying bastard."

Caleb clenched his jaw at the sight of the man slumped on the floor. Blood soaked his shirt and his body lay at an odd angle.

Caleb kicked at the man's feet to see if he was still alive. Not that he cared. Except he might know where his daughter was.

Andrews groaned and opened his eyes, although they were half-slitted and dull as if he was struggling for air.

"You jerk, how could you sell my baby?" Madelyn dropped to her knees and shook him. "Where's Cissy?"

Caleb scanned the room, found the closet and flung the door open, but Cissy wasn't inside. Dammit!

"Where is she?" Madelyn jerked Tim so hard his head flopped back. "What did you do with our little girl?"

"So sorry," Tim muttered on another groan. "Never meant for this to happen."

"What? You didn't intend to get caught?" Caleb barked.

"Not for Cissy to get hurt," he said in a hoarse whisper. "Tried to get her, stop Pedderson, save her."

Madelyn slapped his jaw. "Did he hurt her? Where is she now?"

Tears choked the man, and he coughed, pressing his hand over his bloody chest. "She ran outside… Thought he was coming back for her… Find her…find her, Mad…"

His voice trailed off and he coughed again.

Caleb removed his gun and crammed it against Tim's temple. "Who else was in on this besides Pedderson and Emery?"

Tim's eyes widened, but he blinked as if he wasn't fazed by the gun. He knew he was going to die anyway.

"Mansfield," Tim croaked. "He handled everything.…" He angled his head toward Madelyn. "He hit you with his car, Madelyn. He wanted the money.…"

"That picture in your house," Madelyn said. "Have you been seeing Cissy all along?"

Tim shook his head. "No, I followed Danielle one day and saw Cissy. She never knew I took the picture.…" Tim wheezed for a breath, his eyes bulged then rolled in his head, and his body went slack.

Caleb knelt and felt his pulse, but Tim had just drawn his last breath. But at least he'd given them enough to hang Mansfield.

Madelyn was shaking violently, but she pushed

to her feet and kicked his leg. "I hope you rot in hell."

Then she whirled around, eyes panicked. "Caleb, Cissy's out there somewhere. We have to find her."

Caleb's phone buzzed, and he connected the call.

"Caleb, I'm with Leah and the girls. Sara is upset. She said Cissy is crying and calling to her."

Sweat beaded on Caleb's neck. "Ask her where Cissy is."

He heard Sara crying in the background, Leah consoling her, Gage talking to her. Then Gage came back. "The chicken house," Gage said. "Cissy thought it was a greenhouse. She was looking for sunflowers, but it's empty and dark and she's hiding there."

"Thanks, Gage. Tell Sara she did great." He snapped the phone closed.

"What?" Madelyn clawed at his arms.

"The chicken house," Caleb said. "Cissy thought it was a greenhouse."

"The sunflowers," Madelyn whispered hoarsely. Then she took off running.

MADELYN DASHED OUTSIDE, her heart racing.

Caleb followed on her heels. Three rotting

buildings sat to the right on the hill, the storm swirling snow in a blinding fog as they hurried toward them.

She held her breath as Caleb wrenched open the door to the first one, then stepped inside. It was dark and reeked of chicken feces, but it was empty. They hurried to the second one, the snow pulling at her boots as she waded through the downfall.

Frantic, she shoved tree limbs out of the way to make a path. The rusty door screeched open, the building dark, the stench of chickens lingering in the air. Dirt and straw snapped as Caleb stepped inside, scanning the interior.

Old tools had been stored inside, a wheelbarrow filled with junk, a lawnmower, bags of feed and gardening supplies.

"Cissy," Madelyn called. "Cissy, we're here to save you, honey."

"Sara sent us," Caleb said. "She wants us to bring you home."

Madelyn inched forward, searching behind supplies while Caleb checked the wheelbarrow.

"Cissy," Madelyn said softly. "I'm Sara's mommy. She told me about the sunflowers. She draws them just like you do."

"I know you're scared, Cissy," Caleb said,

walking toward the far end. "But the bad man is gone now. We took care of him and he can't hurt you anymore."

Madelyn thought she detected a movement behind the bags of feed to the right and slowly crept toward it. "Sara wants to play with you, Cissy. She heard you ask her for help, and she wants us to bring you there to see her."

A muffled sound reverberated from the corner behind the feed, and Madelyn's heart raced. But she forced herself to tread slowly, determined not to scare her daughter. Then she rounded the corner and spotted Cissy huddled on the floor with her arms around her knees, her little body trembling.

Tears thickened her throat. Cissy was terrified. She'd witnessed Danielle's murder. Danielle was the only mother she'd known.

And Pedderson had threatened her, stuffed her in his trunk and dragged her away from her home.

"Cissy," Madelyn whispered. "Look at me, sweetheart. I'm Sara's mommy and your birth mommy, too." There would be years to help her understand the truth.

Cissy slowly lifted her little head, her big eyes wide with the horrors of what had happened to her. "You're Sara's mommy?" she asked in a tinny voice.

Madelyn nodded, tears burning her eyes. "Yes. And yours, too. Sara and I got lost from you but that was a mistake. We've been looking for you for a long time, and we want you to come home with us."

Cissy scrunched her button nose, her eyes wary, her lower lip quivering. "I'm scared of the mean man."

Madelyn heard Caleb walk up behind her, his presence offering strength. But he kept his distance, giving them space.

"He's gone now, gone forever. He can't ever hurt you again," Madelyn said in a strained voice. Her heart swelled with love and longing, and she knelt beside Cissy and held out her arms. "Come on, sweetheart. Let's go meet your sister."

Cissy nodded slowly, then lifted her arms, and Madelyn pulled her up against her and hugged her little girl.

She finally had her missing daughter back.

And no one would ever separate them again.

Chapter Eighteen

The next few hours passed in a blur as Caleb contacted the authorities. Tim Andrews's and Rayland Pedderson's bodies were both transported to the morgue. Caleb and Madelyn had given statements to the local sheriff, then Caleb drove Madelyn and Cissy back to Madelyn's.

Gage, Leah and Ruby met them there with Sara.

Caleb's heart clenched as he watched Sara vault from the car. "Cissy!"

Cissy clung to her blanket like a lifeline, but when she spotted Sara, her eyes lit up with a smile and she raced toward her. The girls flew into each other's arms, twirling and swinging each other around as if they'd been waiting for this moment for years.

And they had.

Ecstatic to have both girls safe and reunited, Madelyn's tears flowed freely. She even managed to laugh as she wiped them from her face.

"So Sara was right all along?" Gage asked.

Caleb nodded. "She and her twin have a special connection that saved Cissy's life."

"You saved them," Madelyn said, a look of gratitude warming her face.

He didn't want her gratitude. He wanted her love.

"The authorities caught Mansfield," Gage told them. "Judge revoked his bail, and he'll be going away for a long time."

Caleb sighed. But he'd caused so much damage to so many lives.

Gage and Leah said good-night, then Gage scooped up Ruby and carried her to their car. Caleb watched the happy family, the way Gage protected his pregnant wife, the way he adored his adopted daughter and realized that family was the one thing missing in his life.

The drive back to Sanctuary had been bittersweet. He was happy he'd reunited Madelyn with her daughter, but now the case was over, she no longer needed him.

He needed her though. When he'd seen that man holding the gun to her head, his life had flashed in vivid clarity. He had intended to build a life with Mara and his son.

But that was not to be.

He had been faithful, even loved Mara. Did that mean he couldn't love again?

He did love Madelyn, he realized. He loved her and her girls and he wanted a life with them.

But now was not the time to confess his feelings. Maybe it would never be time. Madelyn needed to be with her daughters, and he didn't have the right to intrude on the family reunion she'd been waiting a lifetime to have.

Besides, he had some things to think through now.

Afraid he would break down and ruin her homecoming with her children by admitting his feelings, he turned and headed back to his car.

Ten minutes later, he found himself standing in front of Mara's grave. Snow littered the grass and tombstone, adding an ethereal touch to the scene as Mara's spirit appeared in front of him, a golden glow shimmering amidst the pristine white.

"I saved them, Mara," he said. "I wish I could have saved you and our son, too."

Suddenly she moved toward him, and he felt a gentle brush of her lips against his cheek. Her image was fading even more, though there was something peaceful and beautiful about her now. "Be happy," she whispered against his ear. "Love the new woman you have found and build a family with them."

He shook himself, certain he had imagined her words, but when he glanced up she was floating away, her hand lifted in a wave, a smile on her face.

She knew he had fallen in love with Madelyn, and she was at peace, moving on into the light.

For a moment, he stood and watched, aching for her and their lost son, aching for Madelyn and her daughters and the life he wanted.

The one he wasn't sure he could have. Or that Madelyn wanted with him.

MADELYN WAS SO EXCITED about having her daughters together and Cissy home that she had barely slept. The only thing that would have made it more perfect was to have Caleb with her. To have him as a part of her family.

But he had his own life.

She woke to the sound of the girls giggling, then they rushed into her room and hopped on her bed. "Good morning, girls," Madelyn said with a beaming smile.

"Morning, Mommy," Sara sang.

Cissy looked a little more hesitant but crawled up and gave her a hug. "Morning."

Madelyn blinked back tears. She had assured Cissy the night before that it was okay that she'd loved her adopted mother, that she could talk about Danielle anytime. She'd also promised they'd take sunflowers to her grave and keep them there year-round.

Then Cissy had told her something disturbing, something she needed to share with Caleb. But first they had to see her mother.

Madelyn winked at the girls. "You know what we need to do today?"

Sara's eyes sparkled. "What?"

"Go see Gran." Madelyn glanced at Cissy, soaking in her features and trying not to let the bitterness over all she'd missed seep into her voice. Cissy was alive and here now. She had to cherish the future, not dwell on the past.

"We gots to get sunflowers for her," Sara said.

Cissy looped her arm through Sara's. "Yep, 'cause sunflowers are the bestest."

An hour later, Madelyn knocked on the door to her mother's unit and found her standing at the door waiting. Her heart overflowed with joy to see her mother standing, then she took a step and more tears flowed.

"Gran, this is Cissy," Sara said proudly.

Madelyn's mother beamed at Cissy and wiped at her own tears as she took the twins by the hands. "We need some girl time," she said and gave Madelyn a pointed look, then gestured toward the kitchen door.

When she glanced up, Caleb was standing in the doorway looking sheepish and wary and more handsome than any man had a right to be.

"Leave the girls with me for a bit, Madelyn. Caleb needs to talk to you."

Madelyn frowned. "I need to talk to him, too."

Her mother grinned. "Go on, then. Sara and I need to show Cissy how we decorate cookies."

"I can help?" Cissy asked.

"Of course." Madelyn's mother pulled her into a hug, and Caleb took Madelyn's hand and led her outside.

He was quiet as he drove, seemingly lost in thought, and her nerves skittered out of control. Then he parked at her house, and remained stony as they went inside.

"Now, what's going on with you, Caleb?" She tossed her jacket on a chair.

He shifted. "You first."

She took a deep breath. "Last night, Cissy talked some about what happened. She said she heard her mommy say something about other missing kids. That's when he killed her."

Caleb frowned. "You mean other phony adoptions?"

"I don't know." Madelyn sighed. "But it makes me wonder if something bigger was going on."

"We'll look into it," Caleb said.

"Is there some problem with my assuming custody of Cissy?"

He closed the distance between them, then gathered her hands in his. "God...no. I'm sorry. I didn't mean to frighten you."

She exhaled in relief. "Then what is it? Why were you at my mother's?"

"I needed to ask her something."

Madelyn frowned in confusion. "I don't understand."

He stroked her arms with his hands. "Just sit down and listen, please."

Madelyn allowed him to guide her to the sofa, then settled on the seat. He joined her, but anxiety lined his face.

"Come on, Caleb. What's going on?"

He sighed wearily, then looked at her, wrestling with his emotions. "You asked me about my family once and I clammed up."

Oh, God, he was married. That was the reason he'd acted so strange. The reason he'd never mentioned the night they'd made love.

She swallowed back the hurt and humiliation. She'd wanted him so badly. "You have a wife?"

He gripped her hands in his. "I had a wife," he said in a gruff voice. "And we were going to have a child, a son, but my wife died."

"Oh, Caleb." Madelyn heard the sorrow and guilt in his voice. "What happened?"

"She was shot by a man who was after me." He paused, gut wrenching. "I should have died instead of them."

No wonder he'd been so tormented when she'd probed into his past. "I'm so sorry.'"

He shrugged. "It was over three years ago, but I never got over their deaths. I blamed myself."

And he still loved his wife. How could he love Madelyn?

"It wasn't your fault," she said simply. "I'm sure she knows that. That she'd want you to move on, to have a happy life."

He looked at her with such torment in his expression that she wanted to cradle him to her chest.

"I didn't believe that I deserved to have a family again," he said brokenly. "To have some-one love me. To move on."

Anguish for him rippled through her. "But that's not true, Caleb. You're a wonderful man. Strong. Protective. Kind. Loving."

His gaze shot to hers and she smiled. "You

are. I saw you with my girls." A blush slowly crept onto her face. "You're also the sexiest, most wonderful man I've ever known. The only man I've desperately wanted in my bed."

Heat flared in his eyes. "I love you, Madelyn. I think I fell in love with you the moment I saw you at GAI that first day."

Shock mingled with joy in her heart. "You did?"

He nodded. "I wanted you then, and I want you now. That's the reason I had to talk to your mother."

She struggled to follow his logic. "I don't understand."

"Since your father is not around, I needed to ask her permission to do this." He lowered himself to one knee, then pulled her hands in his.

Madelyn gaped at him, stunned. "Caleb?"

"Do you love me, Madelyn?"

Good Lord, did she? "Yes. Last night I thought my life was perfect. I had my girls together again, and we were safe. But then you weren't there, and it felt like a piece was missing, that you should have been with us, too."

A slow smile spread on his face, and he reached in his pocket and removed a diamond ring, the simple diamond surrounded by tiny, glittering stones. "Will you marry me, Madelyn, and let me be your husband and the father to your girls?"

Her heart burst with love. "Yes, Caleb. Of course, I'll marry you. I love you with all my heart." She leaned forward, then kissed him tenderly. "And I'd be proud for you to be a father to my girls and to any other little people that come along."

He threw his head back and chuckled, then picked her up and spun her around as he carried her to the bedroom. A second later, they'd stripped and lay curled in each other's arms. His hands and mouth and body loved her in only the way a true friend and lover could do. And when he joined his body with hers, she knew that their union would last forever.

* * * * *

GUARDIAN ANGEL INVESTIGATIONS:
LOST AND FOUND
continues next month with
HER STOLEN SON,
only from reader favorite Rita Herron.
Look for it wherever
Harlequin Intrigue books are sold!

LARGER-PRINT BOOKS!

GET 2 FREE LARGER-PRINT NOVELS PLUS
2 FREE GIFTS!

Harlequin®

INTRIGUE®

BREATHTAKING ROMANTIC SUSPENSE

YES! Please send me 2 FREE LARGER-PRINT Harlequin Intrigue® novels and my 2 FREE gifts (gifts are worth about $10). After receiving them, if I don't wish to receive any more books, I can return the shipping statement marked "cancel." If I don't cancel, I will receive 6 brand-new novels every month and be billed just $4.99 per book in the U.S. or $5.74 per book in Canada. That's a saving of at least 13% off the cover price! It's quite a bargain! Shipping and handling is just 50¢ per book in the U.S. and 75¢ per book in Canada.* I understand that accepting the 2 free books and gifts places me under no obligation to buy anything. I can always return a shipment and cancel at any time. Even if I never buy another book, the two free books and gifts are mine to keep forever.

199/399 HDN FC7W

Name _____ (PLEASE PRINT)

Address _____ Apt. #

City _____ State/Prov. _____ Zip/Postal Code

Signature (if under 18, a parent or guardian must sign)

Mail to the **Reader Service:**
IN U.S.A.: P.O. Box 1867, Buffalo, NY 14240-1867
IN CANADA: P.O. Box 609, Fort Erie, Ontario L2A 5X3

Not valid for current subscribers to Harlequin Intrigue Larger-Print books.

**Are you a subscriber to Harlequin Intrigue books
and want to receive the larger-print edition?
Call 1-800-873-8635 today or visit www.ReaderService.com.**

* Terms and prices subject to change without notice. Prices do not include applicable taxes. Sales tax applicable in N.Y. Canadian residents will be charged applicable taxes. Offer not valid in Quebec. This offer is limited to one order per household. All orders subject to credit approval. Credit or debit balances in a customer's account(s) may be offset by any other outstanding balance owed by or to the customer. Please allow 4 to 6 weeks for delivery. Offer available while quantities last.

Your Privacy—The Reader Service is committed to protecting your privacy. Our Privacy Policy is available online at www.ReaderService.com or upon request from the Reader Service.

We make a portion of our mailing list available to reputable third parties that offer products we believe may interest you. If you prefer that we not exchange your name with third parties, or if you wish to clarify or modify your communication preferences, please visit us at www.ReaderService.com/consumerschoice or write to us at Reader Service Preference Service, P.O. Box 9062, Buffalo, NY 14269. Include your complete name and address.

HILPLI

The series you love are now available in

LARGER PRINT!

The books are complete and unabridged—
printed in a larger type size to make it
easier on your eyes.

Harlequin
Romance

From the Heart, For the Heart

Harlequin
INTRIGUE
BREATHTAKING ROMANTIC SUSPENSE

Harlequin
Presents

Seduction and Passion Guaranteed!

Harlequin
Super Romance

Exciting, emotional, unexpected!

Try **LARGER PRINT** today!

Visit: www.ReaderService.com
Call: 1-800-873-8635

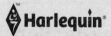

Harlequin®

A *Romance* FOR EVERY MOOD™